SYSTEM CRASH

Slowly the meteor-shaped cars began to climb.

With every yard, Tamsyn found herself gripping the rail in front of her more tightly.

On both sides, the ground below was receding.

Beneath the cars a rhythmic *clunk-clunk* sounded as the metal-toothed track took them up toward the sky.

"Get ready," whispered Rob.

Suddenly the air was filled with screams . . . and everything went black.

INTERNET DETECTIVES

ELECTRONIC MAIL

| File | Edit | View | Options | Window | Utilities | Favelist | Help |

From:
To:

Sent:
Subject:

michael coleman

SYSTEM CRASH

OPEN   SEND   FORWARD   REPLY   DELETE   SAVE   PRINT

Mail:

A SKYLARK BOOK

New York • Toronto • London • Sydney • Auckland

RL 4, 008–012

SYSTEM CRASH

A Bantam Skylark Book/April 1998

Skylark Books is a registered trademark of Bantam Books, a division of Bantam Doubleday Dell Publishing Group, Inc. Registered in U.S. Patent and Trademark Office and elsewhere.

First published 1996 by Macmillan Children's Books, a division of Macmillan Publishers Limited.

Created by Working Partners Limited
London W6 0HE

Computer graphics by Jason Levy
Cover photography by John R. Ward

The right of Michael Coleman to be identified as the author of this work has been asserted by him in accordance with the Copyright, Designs and Patents Act 1988.

ISBN 0-553-48654-3

Bantam Books are published by Bantam Books, a division of Bantam Doubleday Dell Publishing Group, Inc. Its trademark, consisting of the words "Bantam Books" and the portrayal of a rooster, is Registered in U.S. Patent and Trademark Office and in other countries. Marca Registrada. Bantam Books, 1540 Broadway, New York, New York 10036.

PRINTED IN THE UNITED STATES OF AMERICA

CWO 0 9 8 7 6 5 4 3 2 1

CHAPTER 1

Abbey School, Portsmouth, England
Friday, July 20, 1:35 P.M.

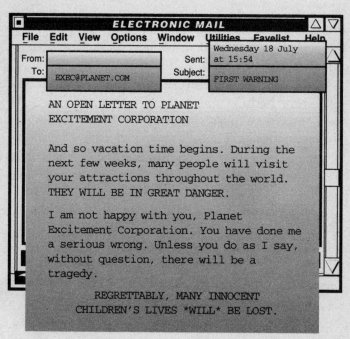

ELECTRONIC MAIL

File   Edit   View   Options   Window   Utilities   Favelist   Help

From:
To: EXEC@PLANET.COM

Sent: Wednesday 18 July at 15:54

Subject: FIRST WARNING

AN OPEN LETTER TO PLANET
EXCITEMENT CORPORATION

And so vacation time begins. During the
next few weeks, many people will visit
your attractions throughout the world.
THEY WILL BE IN GREAT DANGER.

I am not happy with you, Planet
Excitement Corporation. You have done me
a serious wrong. Unless you do as I say,
without question, there will be a
tragedy.

REGRETTABLY, MANY INNOCENT
CHILDREN'S LIVES *WILL* BE LOST.

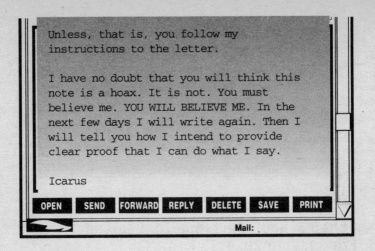

Unless, that is, you follow my
instructions to the letter.

I have no doubt that you will think this
note is a hoax. It is not. You must
believe me. YOU WILL BELIEVE ME. In the
next few days I will write again. Then I
will tell you how I intend to provide
clear proof that I can do what I say.

Icarus

OPEN   SEND   FORWARD   REPLY   DELETE   SAVE   PRINT

Mail: _

Tamsyn Smith, Rob Zanelli, and Josh Allan stared at
the screen openmouthed. It was the most sinister
e-mail they'd ever seen.

As she felt the chill run up her spine, Tamsyn half
wished she hadn't come looking for her two friends in
the Computer Club room but had stayed reading in
the school library.

"Where on earth did you find that note?" she asked.
"The Internet's equivalent of the Chamber of Hor-
rors?"

Josh and Rob laughed, but not very convincingly.

"We were surfing the Entertainment menus," said
Rob. "It was put up as a news flash."

"Very entertaining," said Tamsyn. "Not!"

"It was posted by Interpol," Josh said.

"As in the International Police organization?"

Rob nodded. "It's up in several places, but they

obviously thought putting it under Entertainment would be a good idea. It could be the best way of reaching the people who might be able to help them."

Clicking on the vertical scroll bar, Josh moved back to the previous page. The text that had accompanied the note flicked up on the screen.

```
Interpol is taking the unusual step of
circulating this threatening message on the
Internet and worldwide media because it was
sent over the network to Planet Excitement
Corporation's HQ in Florida, USA. The sender
used an anonymous mail facility to hide his or
her identity.
```

"Anonymous mail?" said Tamsyn. "What's that?"

"There's a way of turning off parts of the routing information," said Rob. "The stuff you get at the front of e-mail messages . . ."

"Like an unsigned letter. They don't have any idea who sent it," chipped in Josh.

"It may be a joke, of course," said Rob. "But the sender's no joker when it comes to using the Net."

"The police aren't treating it as a joke," said Tamsyn, pointing at the screen.

```
Interpol takes this threat very seriously. Any
information that Net users can provide as to
the possible identity of Icarus will be held
in the strictest confidence. Reply by e-mail
to . . .
```

The note ended with the e-mail address of Interpol HQ in Paris.

Josh snorted. "Well, they have to say that, don't they? Even if they do think it's some crackpot with a weird sense of humor."

Tamsyn shivered again. "Just so long as this Icarus *is* a crackpot. How's your Greek mythology, Josh?"

"My what?" said Josh.

"He probably thinks it's the name of a computer game," Tamsyn said to Rob, shaking her head in mock despair.

"Oh, yeah?" Josh clutched the sides of his Abbey School sweatshirt as if he was a lawyer in court. "Icarus. Ancient guy who wants to fly. Makes himself a pair of wings, and off he goes. Trouble is, he gets too near the sun and the wings melt. Wham! He falls to earth. End of Icarus."

"End of discussion!" said Rob. "This is heavy stuff. And it's all I need right now!"

Tamsyn looked at Rob and remembered. "Of course. You're going to Florida for your vacation, aren't you!"

"Next Tuesday. With a visit to the Planet Excitement theme park high on the agenda soon after," said Rob.

Rob's parents, Paul and Theresa Zanelli, ran a successful computer software company called Gamezone. One or the other was regularly flying to the United States on business. This time they'd arranged to combine a business trip to Florida with a three-week vacation. Rob had talked about little else ever since he'd found out.

"That's why we were surfing the Entertainment menu," said Josh. "Rob was showing me the Planet Excitement Web site when we spotted that news flash nearby. The official site didn't mention a thing, of course. Probably worried they'd scare off the tourists."

"We could check it out now," said Rob, looking at his watch. "We've got five minutes before afternoon classes start."

Tamsyn shook her head. "No, it's okay," she said. "I'll wait for the vacation photos."

Josh nodded. "Yeah, me too."

Rob turned to face his two friends. "One of you may not have to wait for those," he said. "One of you will be coming with me, I hope."

Josh and Tamsyn exchanged glances. "You what?" said Josh.

There was a pause. Rob seemed uncertain how to continue. "I wanted to tell you both together," he said finally. "There's been a change of plan. Mom told me this morning." Again he paused.

"Come on, spit it out!" yelled Josh.

Rob took a deep breath. "Okay, it's like this. The plan was to have my cousin Chris come along. To help me, you know?"

As he patted the sides of his wheelchair, Josh and Tamsyn both nodded. Rob had been unable to walk since a car accident had left him paralyzed at age eight.

"Mom and Dad didn't mention the specific reason, but you can guess why."

Tamsyn laughed. Rob didn't need to explain. He was fiercely determined to be treated normally, and always got annoyed if he thought his parents were being overcautious about him.

"Anyway," he continued, "yesterday evening they got a phone call from my aunt Brenda. It seems Chris was playing in a soccer tournament, went in for a shot on goal—and slammed right into the goalie. Result, one badly sprained knee—and no vacation."

He looked from Josh to Tamsyn and back to Josh again. "And that's where you two come in. Mom and Dad agreed that one of you can come with me instead. Assuming you're allowed."

Josh's mouth fell open for the second time that morning. "On vacation?"

Tamsyn's mouth followed suit. "To Florida?"

Rob nodded but didn't smile. "But only *one* of you. Bummer, huh?"

"Which one of us?" asked Josh anxiously.

"To take the place of the soccer-playing Chris?" said Tamsyn with a laugh and a shrug. "Who else? Have a nice time, Josh."

Josh gulped. "Me? Me? Is it me?"

"Sorry, Josh," said Rob. "It isn't." Rob looked at Tamsyn. "Chris is short for Christine. She's been playing soccer for a girls' team since she was ten. Mom thinks a girl would be company for her as well." He looked at Tamsyn. "So, do you think you can come?"

"I—I don't know," stammered Tamsyn, " I'll have to ask. . . . I'll . . . to Florida?"

Josh tapped her on the head. "Hello? Are you receiving him? Yes, to Florida. That's what he said."

Tamsyn's eyes lit up as the news started to sink in. "Yes!" she screeched. "Yes, yes, yes! If I have to tie my dad up and torture him into saying yes, the answer's *yes*!"

As she leaped from her chair and began to bounce around the room, Josh turned to Rob. "Well, she seems real happy about it, I'd say."

Rob looked slightly embarrassed. "I just wish you could come as well, Josh."

Josh shook his head, hiding his disappointment. "No problem. Florida in August? It'll be an oven. Give me a nice cool computer room and endless Net-surfing. . . ."

His face broke into a wide smile. "Hey, there's an idea. With you two out of the way, there'll be no competition for airtime. I can surf all day!"

"Josh . . . haven't you forgotten something?" said Tamsyn as she stopped leaping around the room and settled down on a chair.

"What?"

"This is the last day of classes. The school will be shut for six weeks."

Josh groaned. "No school—no computers. No computers—no Net. Just great!"

Josh's house
Saturday, July 21, 12:25 P.M.

Josh heard the phone ring a couple of times, then stop as his mom picked it up.

He sat up on his bed, ready to dash downstairs if the call was for him. When no shout came from the hallway, he went back to studying the latest issue of a Net magazine.

If I can't get on the Net while Rob's away, then at least I can read about it! he thought.

He was well into an article on smileys when Mrs. Allan poked her head into the room fifteen minutes later.

"Are you getting up at all today?" she asked.

Josh gave the impression it was a tricky question. "Well . . . I suppose so."

"And are you going to see Rob?"

"After lunch," said Josh. "Why?"

"I just wondered," said his mom, closing the door.

It was more than Josh could put up with. Heaving himself out of bed, he threw on some clothes and hurried downstairs.

"Why did you ask if I was going to see Rob?" he asked. A sudden thought struck him. "Was that Rob on the phone? What did he want? Did he say anything about taking me to Florida?"

Mrs. Allan shook her head and laughed. "No, nothing, and no. It was a call for me."

Josh sighed. It was going to be a dull summer.

But then, he hadn't noticed the twinkle in his mom's eye.

Josh pedaled up the smooth blacktop driveway of Rob's house. Leaning his bike against the garage door, he pressed the button on the security intercom at the side of the front door.

Almost at once Rob's voice crackled out of the speaker. "That you, Josh?"

"No, it's a seven-headed alien from the planet Jupiter."

Rob laughed. "Which means you're much better-looking than Josh! Come in!"

The door clicked open with a buzz, and Josh pushed through it into the wide hallway. Mrs. Zanelli came out of the living room to meet him. "Hello, Josh! Come to do some surfing?"

Josh nodded. "Definitely, Mrs. Zanelli. There won't be many more chances for a while."

Mrs. Zanelli smiled. "Oh, I don't know," she said mysteriously, before leaving.

Rob was waiting at the door of his room. "Like the poster?" he said, pointing at the laser-printed sheet taped to the door.

HOME OF ZMASTER

ZMASTER was Rob's user ID on the Net. He'd been surfing longer than any of them, and had his own computer setup. His parents had bought it for him in the days when he wasn't allowed to attend school and was taught at home. It was through using this equipment that he'd first contacted Josh and Tamsyn at Abbey School, and the other friends they e-mailed over the Net. A note from one of them was already on Rob's screen.

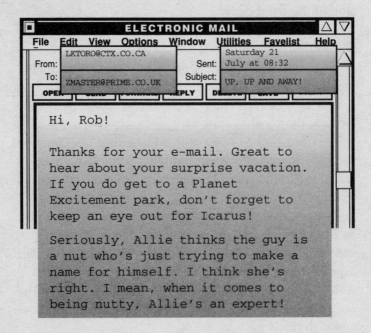

■	ELECTRONIC MAIL	△ ▽
File **Edit** **View** **Options** **Window** **Utilities** **Favelist** **Help**

| From: | LKTORO@CTX.CO.CA | Sent: | Saturday 21 July at 08:32 |
| To: | ZMASTER@PRIME.CO.UK | Subject: | UP, UP AND AWAY! |

OPEN | SEND | FORWARD | REPLY | DELETE | SAVE

```
Hi, Rob!

Thanks for your e-mail. Great to
hear about your surprise vacation.
If you do get to a Planet
Excitement park, don't forget to
keep an eye out for Icarus!

Seriously, Allie thinks the guy is
a nut who's just trying to make a
name for himself. I think she's
right. I mean, when it comes to
being nutty, Allie's an expert!
```

"Allie would probably say the same about Lauren!" laughed Josh as he read the note over Rob's shoulder.

Allie was Lauren's grandmother, Alice. Lauren had lived with her in Toronto ever since Lauren's parents had been drowned in a sailing accident. They were both Net freaks, the difference being that Allie could usually do her surfing only once Lauren had gone to bed.

She's still trying to win crossword
competitions on the Net even though
she hasn't even got one all correct
yet - and if that's not a sign of
nuttiness, tell me what is!

Anyway, Rob, how are you going to
survive being away from the Net for
three whole weeks? There'll be tons
to catch up on when you get back!
Don't forget to send me a postcard.
Unless Allie cracks a competition,
we're going nowhere for the summer.
Boo-hoo!

Lauren :-(for me, :-) for you!

P.S. Still, as you said in your
note, at least somebody'll be
on-line keeping your place warm
for you!

Mail:

"Keeping your place warm?" Josh frowned as he
reached the bottom of the note. "What does that
mean?"

Rob looked up at him. "Like it says. Somebody'll be
keeping my place warm."

"What—here?" said Josh. "Using your PC?"

"Yep," said Rob, straight-faced. Then, when he saw
that Josh still didn't get it, he burst out, "You,
dummy!"

"Me? What are you talking about?"

Rob swung around as Mrs. Zanelli came in with a tray of cookies. "Tell him about the revised plan, Mom. I don't think he's going to believe me if I tell him."

Mrs. Zanelli put the tray down on Rob's desk. As Rob quickly snatched the largest cookie from the pile, she said to Josh, "I phoned your mother this morning and she agreed that you can house-sit for us while we're away."

"House-sit?" said Josh, more confused than ever.

"Okay, Josh," said Rob. "Concentrate. Chris, my cousin, was coming to Florida with us. Aunt Brenda wasn't. . . ."

"She was coming here to look after the house while we were away," said Mrs. Zanelli. "There have been a few break-ins around here lately, and we didn't want to leave the house empty for three weeks."

"It's called house-sitting," said Rob. "Like baby-sitting. Only bigger. Anyway, Aunt Brenda can't do it now, 'cause she'll be Chris-sitting. So Mom and Dad were wondering who could do the job instead." Rob beamed. "And I suggested you!"

"What do I have to do?" asked Josh.

"Just take the mail in every morning," said Mrs. Zanelli, "so that it doesn't pile up inside the door for everybody to see. Look around the place and check that all's well. You won't have to spend the entire day here." She smiled at Rob, then added, "Unless you want to, of course."

"Wh-What . . . You mean . . . ?" stammered Josh.

"Keeping it warm!" said Rob. "I told Lauren you'd

be here, logging on every day. That's what she was talking about!"

Mrs. Zanelli stopped at the door. "So, what do you say, Josh? Will you house-sit for us? Or do I have to look for somebody else?"

"No!" cried Josh.

"No, you can't do it?" teased Mrs. Zanelli, smiling.

"No!" said Josh. "I mean, yes, I can do it! Rob, for the next three weeks I'm gonna keep that machine so warm you'll be able to fry an egg on it when you get back!"

CHAPTER 2

Flight IA241
Tuesday, July 24, 11:05 A.M. (UK time)

"I can't believe it," said Tamsyn. "I mean, I just *cannot* believe it!"

"Try jumping out." Rob laughed. "See if that helps."

Tamsyn looked out of the small window beside her elbow. Far below the Boeing 747 jet they were in, the blue ocean stretched out to the horizon. A small dot of a cruise liner was making a thin white trail across its wrinkled surface.

Less than five hours ago she had been at home, desperately trying to jam her suitcase shut. Since then, the rest had seemed like a dream: passing through the security checks at Heathrow Airport, the loudspeaker calling their flight number, the excitement of boarding the plane first so that Rob could be helped into his seat.

After that, once the other passengers were all on board, there'd been the slow taxi out onto the runway, the short pause while the pilot waited for clearance to take off—and then the jolt of acceleration and the roaring of powerful jet engines as they'd raced down the runway and soared into the air.

"Would you like a drink, miss?"

It took Tamsyn a couple of seconds to realize that the white-shirted flight attendant was talking to her.

"Sorry?"

The man didn't smile. "My name is Carl. I'm part of the cabin staff for this flight to Florida."

"Really!" giggled Tamsyn. "Wow!"

"Would you care for a drink?" Carl waved a hand over the trolley he'd been wheeling down the center aisle as he said in a flat voice, "There's orange juice, tomato juice, Coke . . ."

"Whisky, gin, vodka . . . ," chipped in Rob.

The flight attendant showed no sign of having appreciated the joke, saying, "Only if you're over twenty-one."

"I'll have an orange juice, please," said Tamsyn.

"Coke for me, please," said Rob.

The steward lifted a carton from the trolley. Pouring Tamsyn's juice into a plastic cup, he stretched over Rob and placed it on the small fold-down table in front of her. As he did so, Tamsyn noticed that he had a tattoo on the back of his wrist.

She checked again as Carl poured out Rob's Coke and set it on his fold-down table.

"Anything else you want, just let me know," said Carl dully.

"Funny-looking flight attendant," giggled Tamsyn as Carl moved on down the aisle.

"Maybe he is a she," Rob whispered back, "and they got her to dress up like a man for your benefit!"

"Complete with tattoo?" said Tamsyn. "Now that's what I call a thorough job!"

Rob looked at her. "A tattoo?"

"Didn't you see it?" said Tamsyn. "On the back of his hand. An angel's wing."

A head popped over the back of Tamsyn's seat. "What sort of tattoo would you expect to see on somebody who does as much flying as he must?" said Mr. Zanelli from the row behind. "A parachute?"

Tamsyn and Rob spluttered with laughter. For the rest of the nine-hour flight, whenever Tamsyn saw Carl she couldn't help imagining him floating gently down to earth with a large white parachute billowing out above him.

Manor House
Tuesday, July 24, 11:05 A.M.

At the same time as Tamsyn and Rob were thirty thousand feet up in the air and hurtling toward Florida, Josh was sitting in Rob's room. He'd been there an hour, and was already getting used to the only sound in the empty house being the gentle hum of Rob's computer. He sat back and sighed contentedly.

This was his idea of heaven!

He'd come to Manor House with his mom the day before, so that Mrs. Zanelli could give them a door key and explain how to operate the burglar alarm.

Josh had nodded at every instruction. "We've got to put it on when we leave, right?"

"And *not* set it off when you arrive!" Mrs. Zanelli had said.

"Otherwise I can see the headline," Rob had chipped in. "'House-sitter arrested!'"

But all had gone smoothly. Josh's mom had gone into work late that day, giving him a lift to the house at ten o'clock. At five o'clock she would pick him up on her way home.

All this coming and going will cut down on my surfing time! thought Josh.

As the PC bipped to indicate that an e-mail had arrived, Josh switched into the Mail system.

It was a message from Mitch in New York.

ELECTRONIC MAIL

File   Edit   View   Options   Window   Utilities   Favelist   Help

From: NIGHTOWL@CYBER.COM   Sent: Monday 23 July at 19:59
To: ALLSTAR@ABBEY.   Subject:
OPEN PRIME.CO.UK   WORKERS UPDATE

SEND
FORWARD
REPLY
DELETE
SAVE
PRINT

Hi, Josh! Think of this as a "housewarming" e-mail!

Rob told me about your sitting service, so I thought I'd keep you company. Looks like me, you and Lauren are about the only guys in the universe who aren't jet-setting around the world! Okay, a bit of an exaggeration, but it looks like Tom's gone off-line too. He hasn't been in touch for nearly a week.

Apart from Lauren in Toronto, he, Tamsyn, and Rob regularly contacted Mitch in the United States and Tom Peterson in Perth, Australia. Together, the six of them had solved some pretty amazing mysteries over the Net!

Josh suddenly realized that Mitch was right. Tom hadn't been in touch for a while. Tom's father was a detective in the Perth police and, because of this, Tom was able to provide an endless supply of great facts about criminals and how they went about their dirty business!

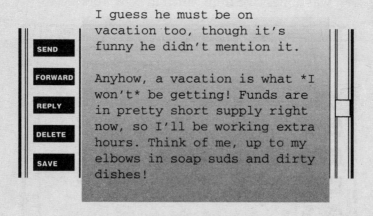

```
                        I guess he must be on
                        vacation too, though it's
    SEND                funny he didn't mention it.

    FORWARD             Anyhow, a vacation is what *I
                        won't* be getting! Funds are
    REPLY               in pretty short supply right
                        now, so I'll be working extra
    DELETE              hours. Think of me, up to my
                        elbows in soap suds and dirty
    SAVE                dishes!
```

Mitch was studying photography in college. To help pay his way, he worked part time at a café called Cyber-Snax, a high-tech place where customers could log onto the Net and have coffee at the same time. One of the perks for Mitch was that Mr. Lewin, his boss, allowed him free airtime.

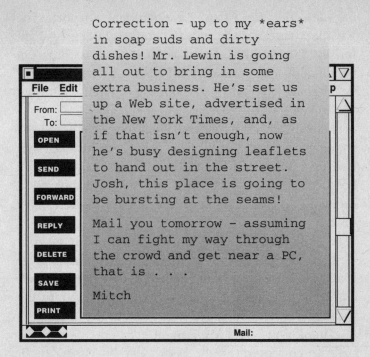

Correction - up to my *ears*
in soap suds and dirty
dishes! Mr. Lewin is going
all out to bring in some
extra business. He's set us
up a Web site, advertised in
the New York Times, and, as
if that isn't enough, now
he's busy designing leaflets
to hand out in the street.
Josh, this place is going to
be bursting at the seams!

Mail you tomorrow - assuming
I can fight my way through
the crowd and get near a PC,
that is . . .

Mitch

Josh grinned. Fighting his way to a PC wasn't going to be a problem for him!

Clicking out of Mail, he went back into Net Navigator, the program that provided menus to help search the Net. Where should he surf to now? *Problems, problems!* thought Josh happily.

Miami International Airport, USA
Tuesday, July 24, 4:35 P.M.

The pilot's voice was cool and clear.

"Ladies and gentlemen, we are about to begin our final descent into Miami International Airport. The weather there is sunny and, at eighty-eight degrees Fahrenheit, nice and hot. Thank you for flying with us. On behalf of my crew and myself I wish you a happy visit."

"Here we go," said Rob, pointing out of the window at Tamsyn's side.

She didn't need to be told. She'd been gazing at the snaking east coast of Florida ever since Mrs. Zanelli had first pointed it out to them. Then it had simply been coastline. Now, as they left the water behind, a highway and the cars speeding along it were clearly visible.

Five minutes later, they touched down with the gentlest of bumps. No more than fifteen minutes after that, Mr. Zanelli was being helped to ease Rob's wheelchair out through the aircraft's exit door and into the passageway, which would take them to the airport.

"Thank you," said Mr. Zanelli.

"Are you going right back, Carl?" Mrs. Zanelli asked the flight attendant.

Carl shook his head. "Layover tonight," he said. "Then back to London tomorrow. After that I'm on the Canada run for a couple of days."

Rob looked at Tamsyn. "Hey, he could drop in and see Lauren!"

"What, wearing his parachute?" she laughed. "Come on, Zanelli, it's vacation time. . . ."

Forty-five minutes later, two cars left the rental car parking lot on the outskirts of the airport.

One, a station wagon, swung northward toward Interstate 95. Mrs. Zanelli was at the wheel, Mr. Zanelli beside her. In the back sat Rob and Tamsyn. Ahead of them was a sixty-mile journey to their hotel right on the edge of the beach at Boca Raton.

The second car, a sedan, turned southward. Soon it would be in downtown Miami.

There, the driver was thinking, he would do what he had promised. At the same anonymous cyber-café he'd used a week before, he would send his next message to the Planet Excitement Corporation. Again, he would sign his name "Icarus."

Yes, it was time for him to make his next move. It was time for him to prove to them that his threat was deadly serious.

little guy and taking the massive profits for yourselves.

So, unless you cooperate with me, some of those profits will disappear. People will stop visiting Planet Excitement parks, because they will be too frightened.

I suspect that you do not believe I can carry out this threat. Therefore, I will supply you with the proof you need. I will cause a major attraction at one of your parks to crash. I will even tell you when! Note well the date, Planet Excitement Corporation.

I WILL STRIKE THIS COMING SATURDAY, JULY 28.

Icarus

| SEND |
| FORWARD |
| REPLY |
| DELETE |
| SAVE |
| PRINT |

Mail:

Toronto, Canada
Wednesday, July 25, 9:05 A.M.

"Allie, you didn't!" cried Lauren King.

Her plump, twinkling-eyed grandmother shrugged

cheerfully. "Okay, so I didn't," she said, holding up a long white envelope. "This is a gas bill."

"You did!" Lauren made a grab for the envelope, but Alice held it out of reach.

"I think there's only one way you'll believe it," she said. "And that's on-line. Go on, go for it."

Impatiently Lauren dived over to the keyboard in the corner of their apartment's small living room.

"Entertainment, Competitions, Prize Crosswords," said Alice, directing Lauren through the menus.

Suddenly there it was. Lauren screeched. "You did! You really did!"

Lauren spun around in her seat. "Tickets? Tickets to what?"

Alice slowly opened the envelope and pulled out a colored leaflet. Holding it close to her face, she peeped inside.

"Hmmm. Remind me, what was it you called me in your note to Rob? Nutty, was it?"

"Joke, Allie! Joke!"

"This nutty old woman has won an all-expenses-paid day of adventure." She pulled a piece of cardboard from inside the leaflet. "And here's *my* ticket!"

Lauren pointed at the screen. "'Tickets,' that says, Allie. Tick-*ets*. You know, as in more than one."

Her grandmother laughed. Dipping inside the leaflet again, she pulled out the second ticket she'd won. Lauren looked at it with mounting excitement.

"Planet Toronto! You've won free tickets to Planet Toronto!"

Lauren punched the air with joy. The Planet Toronto theme park was the biggest in Canada. Not only that, she was about the only one in her class who hadn't been there yet.

"Allie, there are some *awesome* rides there! My friends told me all about them!"

"That's good. Just don't expect me to go on all of them with you, that's all."

Lauren gave her a look. "Allie, you're not going to chicken out on me, are you?" A thought came to her. Planet Toronto was one of the Planet Excitement Corporation's theme parks. "Or maybe you're scared that Icarus isn't nutty, either?"

Lauren ducked as Alice tried to give her a good-natured swipe with the envelope she was holding.

"That does it. I'll show you who's chicken. Every ride you go on, I'll be sitting right beside you!"

"Yes!" shouted Lauren. "Oh, Allie, I can hardly wait. When are we going?"

She looked at the ticket in her hand. It had been stamped at the bottom.

```
VALID ONE DAY ONLY:
SATURDAY JULY 28
```

CHAPTER 3

Manor House
Thursday, July 26, 12:10 P.M.

Josh watched the figure from behind the curtains, unsure about what to do next.

He'd first spotted him fifteen minutes earlier, not long after he'd arrived. Josh had carried the stack of mail from inside the front door to Mr. Zanelli's study, then gone to Rob's room. He'd been about to log on when he'd glanced out of the window.

At first the casually dressed boy had walked slowly past the front gate, and Josh had assumed he was heading for a house further down the road.

But then, when he'd looked out of the window a second time a few minutes later, Josh had seen him outside again—this time looking up at the windows of Manor House.

That was when a thought had caused Josh's heart to jump. *What if he's checking to see if the place is unoccupied? What if he's a burglar, planning to break in?*

Okay, so it was broad daylight. But plenty of break-ins took place during the day, didn't they?

Don't be so stupid! he told himself. *He's probably one of Rob's friends who doesn't know he's gone away.*

Almost at once, Josh ruled out *that* possibility. Rob had been so excited, he'd been telling *everybody* about his trip to Florida. The boy just had to be a burglar!

Flattening his back against the wall, Josh peeked out to examine him more carefully.

About my age, thought Josh, *maybe slightly older. No bigger than me, though. That could be important if he does break in. . . .*

He ducked back sharply as the boy took a hesitant step inside the gate and glanced left and right.

Who is he? Should I call the police now?

If he did call, then they'd want a decent description. Josh peered out again. For a moment he thought the burglar had gone. Then he saw him again. He'd scuttled across the grass and buried himself in the rambling hedge that skirted the opposite side of the Zanellis' front yard. As Josh watched, the boy slowly poked his head out.

He's looking to see if anybody's in the backyard! realized Josh. *That's pretty suspicious-looking.*

Within moments his suspicions were confirmed. Creeping out, the burglar scurried the length of the hedge before disappearing from view. Josh knew exactly where he'd gone. There was a low fence on that side of the house. He was going over it and around the back to see if he could get in that way.

Josh came to a decision. He'd call the police, all right. But only *after* he'd jumped that kid.

Making sure he had the Zanellis' keys in his pocket, he raced down to the hallway. Then, quietly opening and closing the front door, he went out. Crouching low, he dashed along the front of the house.

Carefully he peered around the corner toward the backyard.

There he is! Josh realized excitedly.

The burglar was at the far end, standing and watching, as if planning his next move. Stealthily Josh moved toward him. Thirty feet, fifteen feet, six feet. Then, just as the boy half turned, Josh hit him with a tackle!

"Ooommph!"

The two boys landed on the ground with a thud. "Let go!" yelled the burglar.

But Josh had no intention of letting go. The suddenness of his arrival had given him the edge. Before the boy had a chance to fight back, Josh had pinned him facedown.

"Get off me!" yelled the burglar. "I wasn't up to anything!"

Vaguely Josh realized that the boy's accent wasn't British, but he was in no mood to try and place it. Instead of getting off, as the boy had asked, he grabbed his right arm and twisted it up behind his back.

"If you weren't up to anything," snarled Josh, "it was only 'cause I jumped you in time! What were you gonna do? Break in the back way?"

"I wasn't trying to break in," groaned the boy, spitting out a mouthful of grass at the same time. "I was looking for you!"

"Me?" said Josh.

"Yeah, you! And I might have been sneaking around, and I might have told a few stretchers in my time, Rob Zanelli—but never as big as the one you've been feeding everybody!"

Rob? thought Josh, confused. But as he relaxed his concentration, the other boy wriggled and bucked like a maniac. Before Josh knew it, he'd been flipped over and the boy was kneeling on *him.*

"In a wheelchair? That's one big whopper you've been whizzing around the Net!"

Josh looked up. *Net? Stretchers? Funny accent? And he thinks I'm Rob! Who is he?*

It was Josh's turn to fight back. With a wild lunge, he swung his left fist at the boy's head. It was a beauty. As the left hook thumped him on the ear, the burglar lost his balance and toppled over. In an instant, Josh was free. But so was the burglar! Fists clenched, the two boys knelt facing each other.

"Rob *does* use a wheelchair," snarled Josh. "I'm not him."

"Then who in blazes are you?" shouted the burglar, as if he'd been cheated in some way.

"My name's Josh."

"Josh?" The burglar's fists went down. "Josh Allan?"

Josh didn't relax this time. "Yes, Josh Allan! So who are you?"

The burglar's face broke into a grin. "I'm Tom, you dingbat."

Tom? Suddenly it all fell into place. This kid knew Rob—but didn't know what he looked like. He also knew Josh's last name. And then there was the accent. It couldn't be . . . but it had to be!

"Tom—Peterson?"

The other boy immediately held out a hand. "Internet Detective Tom Peterson," he said at once. "Nice to meet you, Josh. Or as we say in Perth—g'day!"

"But what are you doing here?" asked Josh after they'd dusted themselves off.

"You mean on the other side of the world?" said Tom. "I'm here because of my dad."

"The *other* Detective Peterson, right?" said Josh.

Tom nodded. "That's the one. Anyhow, he came home last week saying he'd been named as a late substitute to go to some crime conference. Mom and I just yawned. He's been to crime conferences before, and they're usually held someplace nobody ever wants to go to. Then he just slips in, really casually, 'This one's an *international* conference. In Southampton, England.' "

"That's only twelve miles away from here!"

"You think I didn't know that? Same goes for Mom. When Dad told us his news, she shot out of her chair. Me, I nearly hit my head on the ceiling! Well, not exactly . . ." Tom rubbed his right ear. "But if I had, it couldn't have hurt much more than your fist."

Josh squinted at Tom's rapidly reddening ear. "Sorry about that. I thought you were a burglar." All the questions that had been buzzing around in his head came pouring out. "Why were you sneaking around, anyway?" he said. "Why didn't you just knock on the front door? Why didn't you tell us you were coming? Why didn't you send an e-mail?"

"Well," said Tom slowly, "at first there was nothing definite. I knew my folks had been thinking about coming to England for years—say, did I ever tell you about our family legend?"

"About the first Peterson being Prisoner 274173, who got shipped out from Portsmouth to Australia back in the year zero?" said Josh. "Yeah, you've mentioned it in e-mails a thousand or so times."

"Anyway," said Tom, getting back to the point, "what I didn't know was that they'd saved almost enough money. Even better, with Dad's fare being paid by the police department, they had enough money to bring me too! So, here I am. We got in a couple of days ago."

"Where are you staying?" asked Josh.

"In Southampton at a little hotel right near the train station. A place called the Sherriot International."

Josh whistled. "It doesn't sound little!"

Tom laughed. "You're right, it's not. It's massive. They even organize day trips. Mom's gone off on a shopping spree to London they organized. So I jumped on a train and came over here."

The Australian boy winked. "She thinks I'm hanging around the hotel, getting over the jet lag. Dad thinks I'm with Mom."

In his e-mails, Tom had spoken more than once about his "stretchers" getting him into hot water. Now that he'd met him, Josh could see why. The thought of e-mails reminded him of his next question.

"But why didn't you send us an e-mail when you *were* certain you were coming?"

Tom waited for Josh to open the front door of Manor House before answering. Then, as Josh led him down the corridor toward Rob's room, he said, "I thought I'd surprise you."

"You sure did!"

"And . . ." Tom hesitated before continuing. "Well, because I didn't know if I'd actually *like* you. I mean, we all send each other notes, but how was I to know if we'd get along when we actually *met*? Anyway, that's why I was checking the place out. If I hadn't liked the look of it, I'd have split, with none of you any the wiser."

Josh had never thought about the Internet in that way before, but Tom was right. When you talked to kids on the Net, you didn't know what they looked like, how old they were, the color of their skin—nothing. That's what made it so great.

But as for actually meeting each other, Tom had a point. Net friends could turn out to be cool—but on the other hand, they could turn out to be absolute weirdos!

"Too late to scoot now, huh?" said Josh, stopping as he reached Rob's door.

Tom grinned. "Yeah. It's okay, though. I guess I can put up with you. For a while," he added, rubbing his ear once more. He looked at the Home of ZMASTER poster on the door. "Let's hope I think the same about Rob and Tamsyn."

Only then did Josh realize what had happened—that Tom had traveled halfway around the world and . . .

"You would if you met them," he said, beginning to laugh. "But they're not here! They're in Florida!"

"Florida!" said Tom. "You mean Florida, as in . . ."

"As in the United States," chuckled Josh. "That's right! They won't be back for three weeks!"

"But I go back home in two!" yelled Tom. He looked at Josh, shook his head, then started laughing himself.

"Looks like you'll have to put up with me," said Josh, opening the door to Rob's room.

Tom eyed Rob's computer setup and whistled. "And you'll have to put up with me!"

Toronto, Canada
Thursday, July 26,
7:35 A.M. (UK time 12:35 P.M.)
Lauren just had to tell somebody! The moment she woke, she leaped out of bed and sprinted into the living room.

Within minutes, her e-mail was winging its way across to Josh.

ELECTRONIC MAIL

File   Edit   View   Options   Window   Utilities   Favelist   Help

From: LKTORO@CTX.CO.CA

To: ALLSTAR@ABBEY.
PRIME.CO.UK

Subject: PRIZE-WINNING
ALLIE!

Hey, Josh! I hope this won't make you feel bad, but I'm off on vacation too!

Okay, so you *do* feel bad. But keep it in check - it's only a day trip. Allie's finally won one of her crossword competitions, and her prize is a couple of tickets to the Planet Excitement park just outside Toronto! We're going on Saturday. I'll send you a full report of what it was like, so you won't feel too left out!

Lauren
P.S. If you don't hear from me, you'll know the dreaded Icarus carried out his threat!

SEND
ORWARD
REPLY
DELETE
SAVE
PRINT

Manor House
Thursday, July 26, 1:08 P.M.

Tom watched as Josh logged in and brought up the e-mail log. There was just one new entry.

"Hey, that's from Lauren!" said Tom. "You gonna look at it?"

Josh opened the note, and together they read Lauren's bubbly note about Allie's crossword prize. Tom leaned forward as he saw the postscript.

```
P.S. If you don't hear from me,
you'll know the dreaded Icarus
carried out his threat!
```

"Icarus?" he said, intrigued. "What's that all about?"

Josh explained about the Icarus note and the news flash from Interpol.

"Yeah?" said Tom. "A real ransom note? C'mon, show me. I'll print it out. I can add it to my crime collection."

"Maybe use it to start a collection of nut cases instead," said Josh as he quit Mail and took the PC into Net Navigator. "This guy has definitely lost a few megabytes of main memory."

Smoothly he traced through to the same point in the Entertainment area that he and Rob had reached before. Again there was an item marked with a News Flash icon.

"Strange," murmured Josh. "I'd have thought it would be old news by now."

The moment he clicked on the icon he saw why that wasn't the case. Interpol had posted another request for help.

```
A second threatening message has been
received by Planet Excitement Corporation
from the person calling himself or herself
Icarus. Once again, Interpol is appealing for
information that may help to identify this
person. . . .
```

Further down the screen, the note from Icarus had been reproduced. Josh and Tom read through it.

"July twenty-eighth," said Tom. "This Saturday." He looked at Josh. "The day Lauren and Allie are going to the Toronto park."

Josh pointed at the Icarus note. "He doesn't say where in the world he plans to strike, does he? And that's assuming he's serious."

"Interpol isn't taking any chances," said Tom.

"I wonder what the Planet Excitement people are doing about it," said Josh. He opened Rob's hotlist of favorite World Wide Web sites and clicked on Planet Excitement. Immediately the screen display switched to the Planet Excitement Corporation home page.

PLANET EXCITEMENT

Planet List

Voyages

Future Launches

Customer Safety

The safety of our customers is our top priority. Each of our parks is totally secure. You can visit us with confidence - and have an experience that is out of this world!

Mail:

"Looks like they're taking it pretty seriously as well," said Tom. "They don't mention Icarus, but there'd be no reason to put up a notice like that otherwise."

"Do you think Rob and Tamsyn have seen this?" asked Tom.

Josh shook his head. "They're like you, Tom—offline. They won't have access to a PC."

"What's the name of the hotel they're in?" asked Tom, reaching for the mouse.

"The Delray Sun, I think," replied Josh.

This time it was Tom who flipped through the Net menus. From the home page he went into Travel, then to Hotels. At the bottom of the screen was a box marked Search For? Tom took the cursor down to it and typed "Delray Sun, Boca Raton."

"Josh, we make a good team," said Tom as moments later the hotel's home page appeared on the screen. There was a Mail Us button in the bottom corner. Tom clicked on it and was immediately taken into an e-mail panel.

Josh began typing.

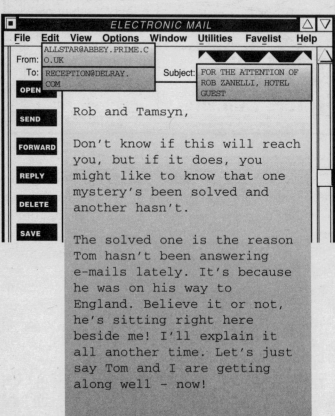

ELECTRONIC MAIL

| File | Edit | View | Options | Window | Utilities | Favelist | Help |

From: ALLSTAR@ABBEY.PRIME.CO.UK
To: RECEPTION@DELRAY.COM
Subject: FOR THE ATTENTION OF ROB ZANELLI, HOTEL GUEST

OPEN
SEND
FORWARD
REPLY
DELETE
SAVE

Rob and Tamsyn,

Don't know if this will reach you, but if it does, you might like to know that one mystery's been solved and another hasn't.

The solved one is the reason Tom hasn't been answering e-mails lately. It's because he was on his way to England. Believe it or not, he's sitting right here beside me! I'll explain it all another time. Let's just say Tom and I are getting along well - now!

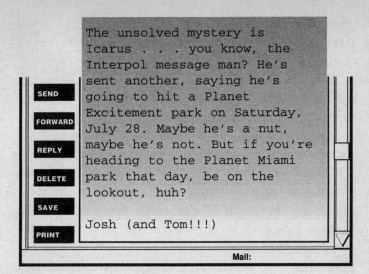

The unsolved mystery is
Icarus . . . you know, the
Interpol message man? He's
sent another, saying he's
going to hit a Planet
Excitement park on Saturday,
July 28. Maybe he's a nut,
maybe he's not. But if you're
heading to the Planet Miami
park that day, be on the
lookout, huh?

Josh (and Tom!!!)

SEND
FORWARD
REPLY
DELETE
SAVE
PRINT

Mail:

"There you go," said Tom. He looked at his watch. "One-thirty. What's that in Florida, half past eight in the morning? They'll be reading it while they have their breakfast!"

Delray Sun Hotel, Florida
Thursday, July 26, 8:32 A.M.

The desk clerk was tired and in a hurry. It had been a busy night, and he was looking forward to going off duty.

There was just one more job he had to do: print out the e-mails that had been received during his shift. Wearily he sat down in front of the PC behind the desk. Opening the mail log, he selected all the new arrivals, then clicked on the Print icon. At the side of the computer, the lights on the front panel of the small laser printer flickered, and individual sheets began oozing out.

The desk clerk began to gather his things together, ready for a quick departure. By the time he was ready, the printer had finished its work.

"Look at all this," he grumbled as he saw the pile of paper waiting to be sorted.

Quickly the desk clerk looked to see who each e-mail was for. Room reservations went into a tray for the staff who would be coming on for the day shift. E-mails for guests he stuffed into the large rack of pigeonholes that covered virtually the whole wall behind him, one pigeonhole for each room in the hotel. They would be picked up by guests when they checked to see if they had any messages.

Working faster and faster, he rattled through the pile. "Rob Zanelli," he muttered as he snatched up the final e-mail in his pile. Quickly he checked the hotel's room allocation directory. "Room four twenty-three."

Hurriedly he stuffed Josh's warning about Icarus into a pigeonhole. In his haste he didn't notice that he'd put it into the pigeonhole for room 424.

It was still there two days later, on Saturday, July 28, as Rob and Tamsyn hurried past the reception desk and out of the hotel to the station wagon in which Mr. and Mrs. Zanelli were waiting to take them to the Planet Miami park.

CHAPTER 4

Planet Miami theme park
Saturday, July 28, 10:10 A.M.

The park was situated north of Miami, a five-minute drive after leaving I-95. Containing dozens of thrilling rides, plus a few gentler ones for those who preferred not to be scared stiff, Planet Miami had been designed to look like the surface of a wild and forbidding planet.

Even the entrance fitted the theme. A massive and constantly changing screen display gave the impression that you were approaching the surface of the planet as you neared the ticket booth.

Tamsyn gave Rob a nudge as the line inched forward. "Come on, don't fall asleep."

"Falling asleep is the one thing I *don't* plan to do," said Rob as he pushed himself another foot closer to the entrance. "Have you seen some of those rides? Look at that one!"

Beyond the entrance, and on both sides, the upper reaches of some of the attractions were visible. It was one of these that had caught Rob's eye, with a chain of rocklike spheres crawling its way up a steep incline.

Tamsyn looked at the plan of the park, which a gruesome-looking character in an alien costume had handed them as they joined the line.

"That must be the Meteor," she said, reading the blurb. "'A blistering hurtle through space ending in a sensational splash landing. Can you hack it?'"

"No prob!" said Rob. He looked up at the ride again. Even from outside the park, the towering Meteor structure looked massive. "It doesn't look as if many others can, though," he said. "There's nobody on it."

Tamsyn saw what he meant. The "meteors" were all empty.

"It must be a safety run," said Mrs. Zanelli beside them.

"A what?" said Rob.

His mom showed them the reverse side of her own park plan. On it was a small notice.

> **FOR YOUR SAFETY**
> *Please note that every attraction at this park*
> *undergoes an hourly safety run.*
> *Your patience at these times is requested.*

"Do you think Icarus knows that?" whispered Tamsyn.

Rob shook his head. "Icarus doesn't even exist. Hey, come on! We're going in!"

Planet Toronto theme park
Saturday, July 28, 10:25 A.M.

Alice saw the yellow blob coming toward her. "You didn't tell me these places came complete with marzipans!"

"Don't you mean Martians, Allie?" giggled Lauren.

"I know what I mean," said her grandmother. "Marzipan's yellow and blobby—just like that thing!"

Lauren laughed again as Allie gave the creature a wide berth, even though it waggled each of its four ears and called out a cheery, "Welcome to Planet Toronto!"

"They're supposed to be aliens," she said. "That's the thing about the Planet parks. They're all designed to look like different planets in outer space."

"Complete with walkie-talkie-carrying aliens," said Allie, looking at the yellow blob. Clipped to its waist was a small black unit with a short aerial sticking out. "Presumably so they can talk alien to each other."

"I bet it's so they can be told where the crowds are. They go on the rides and everything. Lots of kids in my class have had their picture taken standing next to one of them." She smiled mischievously. "Hey, do you want me to take one of you with the blob?"

"No, thanks!" cried Alice. She reached for her camera. "But don't let me stop you. . . ."

"Later, Allie. I want to hit the rides first."

"Which one? The Meteor?"

"Definitely! And Blast-Off," said Lauren excitedly,

"and Lost in Orbit . . ." She reeled off the names of another half-dozen rides, complete with descriptions of what happened when you went on them.

"They sound awful," said Alice, beginning to wish her prize had been something a little tamer, like a crossword dictionary.

Lauren gave her a disgusted look. "You think they sound awful? You ought to be grateful Quantum Leap isn't ready yet, Allie!"

"Quantum Leap?"

"It's the new ride they're working on. It was on their Web page. What happens is they strap you in this—"

"Enough!" said Allie. "Quantum Leap can wait until I win another prize. Let's get on with this one. What do you want to go on first?"

Lauren needed no time at all to make up her mind. "The Meteor," she said at once.

Planet Miami theme park
3:25 P.M.

"Haven't you two had enough yet?" asked Mrs. Zanelli outside the park's central refreshment area.

Rob and Tamsyn looked at each other. "Nah!" they said in unison.

"I've just got to go on the Meteor again," said Rob. "That ride is *wild*!"

"Well, wild for your old dad is an ice-cold beer," said Mr. Zanelli, sinking down onto a chair. "We'll see you back here. And be careful."

"Don't worry, Dad," laughed Rob. "Tamsyn will stop me from rolling under a runaway alien!"

They headed off once more toward The Meteor. . . .

Planet Toronto theme park
3:28 P.M.

"I am going on that again!"

Lauren shook her head in amazement. Why hadn't she realized before that although Allie was old on the outside, inside she was just a little girl?

"Allie, the Meteor isn't the *only* ride in the park, you know!"

"I know," said her grandmother. "But it's the one I like best. So are you coming on again, or not?"

Lauren looped her arm into Allie's. "Of course I'm coming! You think they'll let a little old lady like you go on the Meteor all by herself?"

Planet Miami theme park
3:43 P.M.

Tamsyn and Rob had to line up again, but they didn't mind. Apart from the fact that the Meteor was a ride that catered to wheelchair users—Rob was able to slide from his seat straight into a meteor car—it was a heart-stopping experience.

Each train of cars could hold about thirty people. The cars were ball-shaped at the front, with the metal pitted and cratered like a real meteor, but open-sided all the way along. Once they picked up speed, bolts of blinding light streamed back the whole length of the cars, giving them the feeling that they really were riding the tail of a meteor.

Not surprisingly, they had to wait on line for fifteen minutes or so. But finally they were aboard.

"Seats in the back!" crowed Rob, fastening his safety harness. "This is going to be the best yet!"

There was a short wait as the remaining seats filled up. Then, slowly, the cars began to climb.

Tamsyn found herself gripping the rail in front of her more tightly.

On both sides, the ground below was receding. The people looking up at them were getting smaller and smaller.

Beneath the cars a rhythmic *clunk-clunk* sounded as the metal-toothed track took them up toward the sky.

"Get ready," whispered Rob.

Suddenly the air was filled with screams . . . and everything went black.

Planet Toronto theme park
3:45 P.M.

"Oh, no!"

Lauren groaned with disappointment as she heard the announcement over the loudspeaker.

"There will now be a safety run on this attraction. The next ride will take place shortly. Please be patient."

"It *would* have to be just as we got to the front of the line," said Lauren.

"We won't have to wait long," said Allie. She looked around. "Say, why don't we get that alien picture now? How about standing next to Silver over there?"

Among the people pouring out of the meteors that had just pulled in was a character dressed in a shiny silver tunic and pants. He had a high-browed silver mask completely covering his face, and matching silver gloves. A black box with an aerial was attached to his waistband.

"Okay," said Lauren. "I don't know what he's supposed to be, though."

As Allie reached for her camera, Lauren hurried across to Silver. He'd moved away from the ride entrance and was standing away from the crowds.

"Excuse me. Is it okay if I have my picture taken with you?"

Silver looked down. "Not now, kid."

But Allie already had her camera up to her eye. "I can't tell if he's smiling, Lauren, but you're not. Ready . . ."

As the shutter clicked, Silver moved sharply away from Lauren's side.

"I guess he's camera-shy," said Allie when Lauren told him what Silver had said.

"He shouldn't be," said Lauren. "Not working here."

She didn't think any more about it as, behind them, the Meteor began its test run.

Planet Miami theme park
3:44 P.M.

As the meteor slid into the blackness and they heard the first screams, Tamsyn and Rob both felt like screaming themselves. But it was more fun not to.

Momentarily the cars stopped. Then, slowly, they began to pick up speed. As they accelerated, the cars angled over to one side, then spun over to the other side.

The laser lights came on, streaming past them as they went faster and faster. Suddenly they left the blackness and were out in the daylight. The meteor pitched forward and thundered down, like a real meteor plummeting into the sea.

Faster and faster they went until, with a tremendous splash, the cars hit the water at the bottom of the track . . . and gently glided to a halt.

"That was great!" cried Rob as the attendant brought his wheelchair over. "Come on, Tamsyn. If we're quick, we can go on a third time."

Planet Toronto theme park
3:48 P.M.

Lauren and Allie saw the flash of fire moments before they heard the explosion.

One minute they'd been watching the empty meteor winding its way up toward the tunnel at the highest point of its journey.

The next, from just inside the mouth of the tunnel, a sheet of red flame spurted out. Immediately after came the muffled roar of the explosion—and then the screams started for real.

Thrown from its track, the meteor started to topple sideways. Horrified, Lauren and Allie saw the front part of the train, already inside the tunnel, jam fast as the cars hit the wall. But there was nothing to hold the rear portion, which continued to topple sideways, over the edge of the track.

For a moment it swung high in the air. Then, with a sudden tearing of metal, the end section of the meteor ripped free and plunged to the ground.

As frightened people began running in all directions, Icarus turned and walked slowly away.

The test had worked perfectly. Now they would believe him when he sent his next message.

That would have to wait until he got to London. No matter. They would know now that he had carried out his promise. They would be waiting for him to write again.

Icarus allowed himself a satisfied smile—a smile that was unseen beneath his silver mask.

CHAPTER 5

Manor House
Sunday, July 29, 11:27 A.M.

"Close call," whistled Josh. He and Tom were reading the note Lauren had fired off the moment she and Allie had returned to their apartment.

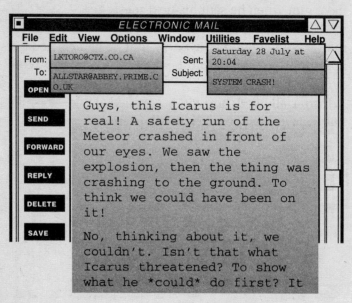

ELECTRONIC MAIL

File   Edit   View   Options   Window   Utilities   Favelist   Help

From: LKTORO@CTX.CO.CA
To: ALLSTAR@ABBEY.PRIME.CO.UK

Sent: Saturday 28 July at 20:04
Subject: SYSTEM CRASH!

OPEN
SEND
FORWARD
REPLY
DELETE
SAVE

Guys, this Icarus is for real! A safety run of the Meteor crashed in front of our eyes. We saw the explosion, then the thing was crashing to the ground. To think we could have been on it!

No, thinking about it, we couldn't. Isn't that what Icarus threatened? To show what he *could* do first? It

seems to me he must have
aimed to sabotage a safety
run, just to prove his point.

"Maybe this Icarus kook has sent another message,"
said Tom. "Let's check after looking at this, okay?"

"Okay," said Josh.

According to the news
bulletins, the experts have
already determined how it was
done. They believe it was a
tiny magnetic device planted
on the track and set off by
remote control. The Meteor
cars almost stop when they
get in that tunnel. Icarus
must have carried the device
on the ride himself and
leaned out to attach it to
the track when the cars
slowed. Then, when the safety
run took place, he set it off
by remote control.

That's the *really* scary
thing. We were watching that
run, so he could have been
standing right there with us!
Still, don't let me put you
guys off. Apart from Icarus
and his explosion, it was a
cool day!

Lauren :-$ (a "shaken"
smiley!)

| OPEN |
| SEND |
| FORWARD |
| REPLY |
| DELETE |
| SAVE |
| PRINT |

Mail:

"Too bad they didn't see anything suspicious," said Josh. "We could have done some Internet detecting."

Tom grinned. "Yeah." He suddenly looked thoughtful. "Hey, maybe they *did* see something suspicious, but just didn't realize it."

"Like what?"

"I overheard a couple of the conference people on the bus coming over this morning."

After giving him a good talking to for his solo excursion to Portsmouth, Mr. and Mrs. Peterson had forbidden Tom to set foot outside the hotel without them. They'd softened a bit when he'd told them about how Josh was his best friend on the Net. Finally they'd given in completely when Tom had pointed out the Portsmouth Historic Ships excursion the conference organizers had arranged for that day and said that if he went on it, his parents would not only know where he was, but could arrange for the bus driver to drop him off near Manor House as well!

"Apparently," Tom went on, "the police don't always get a good response to their calls for information because the public looks for the wrong things. Why don't we fire a note back to Lauren? Ask her to tell us everything she and Allie saw while they were at the Meteor."

Josh hesitated. "You're serious, aren't you?"

"Sure I'm serious," said Tom.

"You really think we've got a chance of tracking down Icarus? Come on, Tom, we know nothing about him!"

"You're wrong." Tom ticked off points on his fingers as he said, "One, we know he was in Toronto yesterday. Two, we know he's got a grudge against the Planet Excitement Corporation. Three, he knows his electronics. And four, he's on the Net."

"On the Net? How'd you work that out?"

"Because he's sending his warnings by e-mail, of course."

"But," argued Josh, "he's doing it anonymously. He could have walked into any old cyber-café and done that."

"Without knowing enough to be sure he could e-mail them in the first place?" Tom shook his head. "No way. He's out there on the Net, all right."

Josh nodded slowly as the suggestion sank in. "So if *he's* on the Net . . . and *we're* on the Net . . ."

"There should be some way we can nail him!" said Tom brightly. "All we've got to do is pick him out of a zillion users!"

He got to his feet. "Anyway, come on. That's enough surfing for now. My folks have given me some money for a good old British fish-and-chips lunch. After that, we're going to Portsmouth Harbor. I want to see where my ancestor got shipped out from before I catch that bus back."

Josh held up a hand. "Hang on. One more minute." Lauren's note was still on the screen. He clicked on Forward, typed a little message on the end of it, then filled in the address boxes.

"Just trying Rob and Tamsyn again," he said, his

steady smile fading as he added, "Just in case Icarus is heading their way."

Delray Sun Hotel, Florida
Sunday, July 29, 6:40 P.M.

Rob received both of Josh's messages together, when they got back from the long drive to the Keys, the archipelago of islands at the tip of Florida.

"I am sorry," said the desk clerk as he handed them over. "One of them was put in the pigeonhole for room four twenty-four by mistake. I only found it when I checked a guest into that room a little while ago."

As Mr. and Mrs. Zanelli headed up to their room, Rob and Tamsyn went off to a quiet corner of the hotel lobby to read the e-mails.

"Tom's in Portsmouth?" cried Tamsyn as she read the first. "Why didn't he say he was coming over?"

"Why?" said Rob. "Would you have passed up this trip and stayed behind to see him?"

Tamsyn pretended to think for a moment. "Nope," she laughed.

"Anyway," said Rob, "he and Josh seem to be getting on pretty well without us." He turned over the second e-mail.

"That was pretty close," said Tamsyn as they read through the note from Lauren that Josh had forwarded. "This Icarus guy must be a fruitcake."

They then read what Josh had added.

```
Tom thinks this Icarus is a Net user. We
might just surf around, see if we can pick
up any clues. In the meantime, you two be
careful.


At least Icarus isn't threatening to sink
anything, so we'll be all right. Tom's
dragging me off to look at the historic
ships in Portsmouth. I told him none of
them is the prison ship used to cart his
evil ancestor to Australia, but he doesn't
believe me!

Josh and Tom
```

"Tom and his family legend," chuckled Rob. He looked across to the desk clerk behind the counter. "Hey, I wonder if he'll let us reply to these."

The desk clerk frowned when they asked him. "You'll get me hung," he said quietly, "but I guess we owe you for making you wait." He pointed down a corridor. "Go down to room seventeen. It says 'Business Suite' on the door. There's a PC in there that's connected to the Net. You can use the ID GUEST_X, okay? But no hogging it. Any other guest turns up to use it, that's it—log off. You read me?"

"Sure," said Rob, giving a thumbs-up sign. He spun around and headed for room 017. They were in luck. The room was empty.

He clicked on Mail. When the message screen came up, the From: ID was already filled in as

GUEST_X@DELRAY.COM. "They'll probably guess it's from us," Rob said with a smile. He started typing.

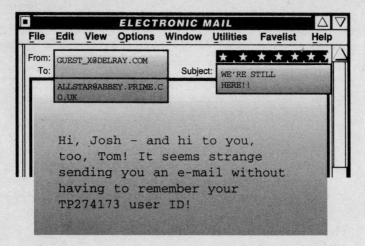

"Just out of curiosity," said Tamsyn, "why does he use that weird ID? Do you know?"

"Easy," replied Rob. "*TP* for Tom Peterson. And *274173* from the Peterson legend."

Tamsyn gave him a bemused look. "You've lost me."

"That was supposed to be his deported ancestor's prison number. Tom thinks the poor guy had it tattooed on his leg!"

Perhaps it was the combination of the e-mail in her hand, the talk of legends, and Rob's mention of the word *tattoo*; Tamsyn didn't know. But a sudden thought came into her mind.

"That flight attendant on the plane. Carl. That tattoo on the back of his hand. Wings, remember?"

"Instead of a parachute," said Rob with a grin. "So?"

"Icarus. In the legend, he wore a pair of wings. And fell to earth—just like that meteor ride he sabotaged."

This time Rob laughed out loud. "Come on, Tamsyn. Get real! There must be a zillion people with tattoos like that!"

"Going to Toronto?" said Tamsyn quietly.

"Huh?"

"Remember what he told your mom as we got off the plane? He said he'd be on the Canada run this weekend. He *could* have been there."

Rob shook his head. "Tamsyn, that's crazy!"

Tamsyn thought for a moment—and snorted in agreement. "It is, isn't it? Even for me!"

Minutes later, their reply to Josh and Tom was on its way.

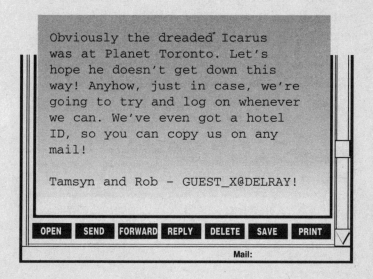

```
Obviously the dreaded Icarus
was at Planet Toronto. Let's
hope he doesn't get down this
way! Anyhow, just in case, we're
going to try and log on whenever
we can. We've even got a hotel
ID, so you can copy us on any
mail!

Tamsyn and Rob - GUEST_X@DELRAY!
```

OPEN   SEND   FORWARD   REPLY   DELETE   SAVE   PRINT

Mail:

Cyber-Snax Café, New York
Sunday, July 29, 7:05 P.M.

"I'm leaving now, Mr. Lewin," called Mitch. "See you in the morning."

Mitch's boss looked up from his cluttered desk in the small back room he used as an office.

"Sure, Mitch. Bright and early, okay? Handout day tomorrow."

"Handout?" said Mitch, frowning.

Mr. Lewin leaned down to haul a large box up from the side of his desk. It was full to the brim with colorful sheets of paper.

"Handout, shmandout," said Mr. Lewin, smacking himself on the side of the head. "I mean handbills."

Now Mitch understood—and he groaned. He'd hoped Mr. Lewin's idea of giving out Cyber-Snax handbills to people in the street would have been forgotten. But, looking at the boxful of bright orange sheets, he knew that hadn't happened. His boss pulled one from the box and handed it over.

"So, what do you think?" asked Mr. Lewin. "Will it bring in the business?"

Mitch held the fluorescent sheet at arm's length. "It'll sure get us noticed, Mr. Lewin!"

"So you do like it." Mr. Lewin beamed. "Great! Because that's what you'll be doing all next week, Mitch. Giving them out!"

Flight IA434, London to New York
Monday, July 30, 11:30 A.M.

Icarus felt happy. Everything was proceeding according to plan. The Toronto test had worked perfectly. He knew it. What was more, the Planet Excitement Corporation knew it.

He had told them as much in his third message, keyed in that morning from a PC in an Internet café he'd discovered in London. It had been the shortest message so far.

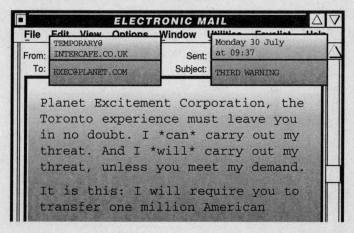

ELECTRONIC MAIL

File   Edit   View   Options   Window   Utilities   Favelist   Help

From: TEMPORARY@INTERCAFE.CO.UK
To: EXEC@PLANET.COM
Sent: Monday 30 July at 09:37
Subject: THIRD WARNING

Planet Excitement Corporation, the Toronto experience must leave you in no doubt. I *can* carry out my threat. And I *will* carry out my threat, unless you meet my demand.

It is this: I will require you to transfer one million American

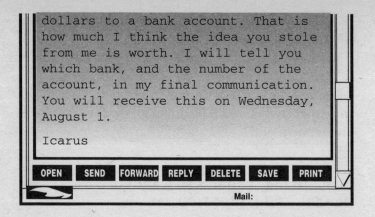

```
dollars to a bank account. That is
how much I think the idea you stole
from me is worth. I will tell you
which bank, and the number of the
account, in my final communication.
You will receive this on Wednesday,
August 1.

Icarus
```

| OPEN | SEND | FORWARD | REPLY | DELETE | SAVE | PRINT |

Mail:

There had been only one problem. The café's system hadn't allowed him to turn off the routing information. So they would know where he'd sent the message from. But that would be all they'd know.

Everything else would be as undetectable as before. And the next message, his final message, would be sent from an Internet café on the other side of the Atlantic.

Icarus looked at his watch. If the flight was on time, they would be landing in New York in three hours.

Sherriot International Hotel, Portsmouth
Monday, July 30, 1:30 P.M.

Tom met Josh at Southampton Central station. From there it was just a short walk to the hotel where the Petersons were staying. They found Tom's parents sitting at a round table on the hotel patio.

"Nice to meet you, Josh," said Mr. Peterson after Tom had done the introductions.

"Tom's told us all about you," said Mrs. Peterson. "And about your house-sitting!"

"It's the coolest way of staying on-line during vacation," said Tom enthusiastically. "When we get back home I'm planning to put an ad in our local paper!"

"Saying what?" asked Mr. Peterson.

"PC-sitting service!" said Tom. "Responsible young man willing to look after your PC while you're away! Screen wiping and e-mail checking my specialty!"

"You *are* joking, Tom—aren't you?" said Mrs. Peterson.

Tom merely smiled. His parents seemed in a good mood. It was time to strike. "Changing the subject . . . Josh's mom says I can crash at their place for a couple of days. How about it?"

"Tom," growled Mr. Peterson, "if you're making this up . . ."

"No way, Dad!"

"It's true, Mr. Peterson," said Josh. He held out the note his mom had written that morning.

"Official invite." Tom grinned. "What do you say? We'll come back in time for the trip on Friday."

Mr. Peterson smiled as he got to his feet. "It's okay by me, Mary. Josh might teach him a few things about computers." He clapped a hand on Tom's shoulder. "Just in case I want to be your first PC-sitting customer, son."

Tom looked up at his dad, wide-eyed. "You mean—

we're getting a PC? No more trips to school while Mom's cleaning? We're going to be on the Net at home?"

"Hold on, not so fast. I'm thinking about it." Mr. Peterson lifted his blue conference folder from the table and tucked it under his arm. "We had a session this morning about computer crime," he said, patting the folder. "It's growing all the time. Viruses, time bombs . . ."

"Blackmailers like Icarus," said Tom.

Mr. Peterson looked sharply at his son. "You know about him?"

"Sure. We've seen his notes on the Net."

"Do you know he's sent a third?"

Josh and Tom exchanged glances. "When?" said Josh.

"This morning," said Mr. Peterson. "This time it was traced. He sent it from a cyber-café in London." He looked at his wife. "It's made the conference organizers have second thoughts about their end-of-conference trip on Friday, I can tell you."

"Trip?" said Tom. "What trip?"

Mr. Peterson got ready to go. "It's traditional, apparently. After the conference ends, the delegates and their families go out somewhere for the day. We wondered if Josh would be able to come as well, to keep you company."

"Yes, he would!" said Tom, before Josh could open his mouth. "Where?"

"Planet London," said Mr. Peterson. "It's the Planet Excitement park in England."

CHAPTER 6

Manor House
2:39 P.M.

They caught the train back to Portsmouth right after lunch, logging onto the Net the moment they reached Manor House.

"What if Icarus turns up next Saturday," bubbled Tom, "and we nab him at Planet London? Wouldn't that be something?"

"Tom, get real. We're looking for one man in a zillion. And you heard what your dad said. He sent his third message from a cyber-café. Doesn't that mean Icarus isn't on the Net himself?"

"Of course it doesn't," said Tom. "If you ask me, it's more likely to mean he *is* on the Net. It's his way of making sure he isn't spotted—you know, like a bank robber wearing a stocking over his head so he isn't recognized!"

On Rob's PC, the Net search they'd set in motion ended. Up flashed Interpol's latest request for further information, together with the third note from Icarus.

That is how much I think the idea you stole
from me is worth. I will tell you which bank,
and the number of the account, in my final
communication.

"Well, that's why he's blackmailing them, anyway,"
said Josh. "He believes they've stolen one of his ideas."

"Right," said Tom. "But what sort of idea is worth a
million dollars?"

Josh thought about it. What sort of idea *would* be
worth a lot of money? How did theme parks make
their money, anyway? The answer to that was simple.
The more customers they got, the more entrance
money they collected.

"It can only be an idea that got more people paying
to go to Planet Excitement parks," he said. "But what?"

"Rides!" exclaimed Tom at once. "That's what gets
kids into parks like that. New rides! Haven't you noticed how they seem to launch a new ride every year?"

"So—one of their rides could have been an idea
Icarus sent them? One they used?"

"Right. And he feels they should have paid him for
it."

"The Meteor," said Josh. "That was the ride he sabotaged. Maybe that was the one he invented. . . ."

Even as he said the word, Josh was sliding the
mouse across to bring back the Net Navigator home
page. Clicking on Science, he brought up the next level
of menu. It had a number of entries, spreading over a
couple of screens. Josh scrolled down until he reached
the one he was looking for.

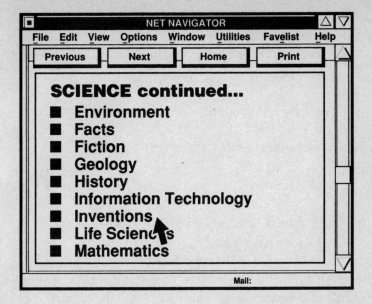

SCIENCE continued...

- ■ **Environment**
- ■ **Facts**
- ■ **Fiction**
- ■ **Geology**
- ■ **History**
- ■ **Information Technology**
- ■ **Inventions**
- ■ **Life Sciences**
- ■ **Mathematics**

Mail:

"Inventions?" said Tom as Josh clicked on that menu item. "Where's that going to get us?"

Josh started to explain his thinking. "If Icarus is an inventor, which is what it looks like—"

Tom realized where Josh was headed. "Then maybe he's come up with other ideas. And posted them on the Net."

"You got it!" said Josh, his face alight—until he looked at the list that had just appeared on the screen. "Six hundred entries!" he cried as he saw the total at the head of the list. "Is everybody in the world an inventor?"

They began scrolling down the list. Starting with "Alarm for a fishing rod—snooze happily, this alarm sounds when you've caught a fish!" the list contained all kinds of wild and wacky ideas. They stopped as they reached "Beer flavoring—just add to water for a delicious beer-flavored drink. Makes wonderful ice pops."

"We'll be here forever. Can't we use a search and narrow it down?"

At the bottom of the screen was a panel.

SEARCH FOR?

Josh moved the cursor to the box—and paused. "What *do* we search for?"

Tom shrugged. "Theme park?"

Josh typed in the words. Impatiently they waited until the search was complete. As the result was flashed on the screen, they groaned. The search had found nothing.

"Zilch," said Tom. "Try 'ride' instead."

"Yeah!" said Josh as the search returned three successful matches. But his excitement disappeared quickly as they looked at them.

1. Safer bike **ride**s with these anti-skid bicycle brakes. (Author: <u>Jim Lake</u>)

2. **Ride** your horse in comfort with this new saddle. (Author: <u>Barbara Meek</u>)

3. Hovercars. Bumpy **ride**s could be a thing of the past with a car that works like a hovercraft. (Author: <u>Carl Russell</u>)

"Nothing like it," said Josh. "Not even worth look-ing at."

Disappointed, they flipped back to the Science menu. "Why not try the search on 'Science Facts'?" said Tom. "That might turn up a few clues."

Josh shook his head. "No, I think we're heading nowhere here," he said, without really concentrating, as he moved the cursor upward and clicked.

"We're *definitely* getting nowhere with that search," said Tom. "You clicked on 'science fiction,' not 'science fact.' All that'll give you is a bunch of articles about rides on UFOs!"

"I'll scrap it," said Josh as their search ended. It hadn't drawn a complete blank, but the one entry it had found looked pretty useless.

```
1. Could you ride in a flying saucer? (Author:
   Carl Russell)
```

"No, hang on," said Tom. "Look at the author. Didn't he have something under Inventions as well? The hovercar or something?"

"So he gets around," said Josh. Still, he clicked on the item anyway.

```
People who are scornful about UFOs argue that
flying saucers couldn't possibly fly. I don't
see why not. A hovercraft is the same shape,
and it floats on water and over the ground. I
have come up with a design for a hovercar,
which would be much more maneuverable than an
ordinary car.
    It all has to do with air pressure. I fly on
```

airplanes a lot. When there's turbulence, the
air pressure can fall dramatically for an
instant. When this happens, the plane drops
like a stone until it reaches another layer of
air dense enough to hold it up. I think this
is how a flying saucer could work. I'm
starting to design one. I will post details on
the Net when I've finished it.

   To begin with, I'd like to see a small one
built. It could carry a few people, and just
go straight up and down. A fun idea I've had
is that it could make a really good theme-park
ride — a flying saucer that floats slowly
upward, then shoots back down again, stopping
on a cushion of air just before it crashes! I
think kids would love it.

                                   Carl Russell

"Carl Russell," murmured Josh. He wrote the
name down. "You don't think he could be the guy, do
you?"

But Tom wasn't listening. He was busy flipping
through the leaflet about Planet London that Mrs. Peterson had given them at lunchtime.

"There *is* a flying saucer ride!" he cried. "Listen:
'Are you brave enough to handle it? Whistle around in
circles with this death-defying ride!'"

Josh frowned. "It doesn't sound like the one this
Carl Russell described."

Tom waved his hands. "Aw, who cares? If he's a nut,
it doesn't matter. He could think they've stolen his
idea anyway." He leaned closer to the screen. "Hey, his
name's underlined. That means there's a link to some
other info, doesn't it? Come on, Josh, hit it!"

Josh moved the cursor onto the name. At once it changed its shape to a pointing finger. Josh clicked once.

Tom whistled as a new screen came up. It carried a page of biographical details about Carl Russell, complete with a scanned-in color photograph of a slim, fair-haired man.

"Wow, he is a Net buff. He must have put this up himself."

"Yeah, I've seen a few like it while I've been surfing. It's getting a lot more common."

They read the details together.

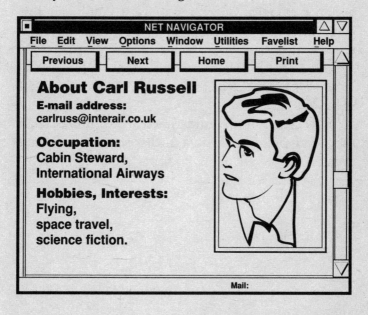

I've been on the Net for about four years now. I subscribe to over twenty newsgroups, although my favorites are those to do with flying and the conquest of outer space.

I think space exploration has brought about many benefits. I'm certain there's life on other planets, and think it's very likely that Earth has been visited by UFOs. I read a lot of science fiction books, and you could well bump into me at meetings of the Science Fiction Society.

My job takes me all over the world. That might sound exciting, but I hate it. My dream is to be able to stay at home and work on my inventions. My job also means I'm not always able to reply at once to e-mail messages. Check my <u>diary</u> if you haven't received a reply to an e-mail you've sent—it could show that I'm away.

"Click on that!" said Tom at once. "Let's have a look at his diary."

Josh clicked on the underlined word. Immediately they were presented with a further screen of information.

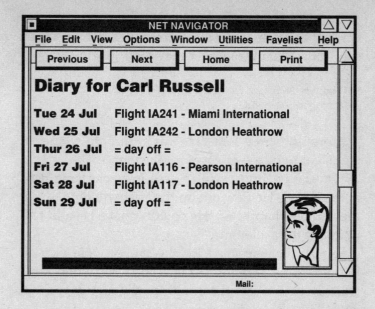

NET NAVIGATOR

File Edit View Options Window Utilities Favelist Help

| Previous | Next | Home | Print |

Diary for Carl Russell

Tue 24 Jul	Flight IA241 - Miami International
Wed 25 Jul	Flight IA242 - London Heathrow
Thur 26 Jul	= day off =
Fri 27 Jul	Flight IA116 - Pearson International
Sat 28 Jul	Flight IA117 - London Heathrow
Sun 29 Jul	= day off =

Mail:

"Is that all?" said Tom glumly as he saw it. "I was hoping there'd be a lot more detail."

"What?" said Josh. "Like 'Saturday, July 28. Sabotage ride at Planet Toronto park'?"

Tom gave a wry smile. "Yeah, something like that." He pointed at the screen. "Anyhow, on Saturday this guy was taking off from Pearson International, wherever that is."

"You want to check?" said Josh.

"Don't see much point," said Tom. "You can't sabotage a ride from thirty thousand feet up in the air, can you? Well, check anyway. At least we'll learn something."

Josh came out of Carl Russell's diary and went back

to the Net Navigator start page. Within moments he'd worked through Travel to Airports. A search on "Pearson" gave them the answer they were looking for.

```
Lester Pearson International Airport –
Toronto, Canada.
```

"Toronto!" cried Tom. "He was in Toronto! Come on, that's got to be too much of a coincidence."

"On the twenty-seventh," said Josh, checking back at the diary. "He flew out on the twenty-eighth, when the accident happened. He couldn't have been in two places at the same time."

Eagerly Tom reached for the mouse. "He was on flight IA one seventeen. Let's check that one out." Quickly he navigated through to the Net pages that gave flight schedules.

"It didn't leave until after seven in the evening," said Josh. "So he *could* have been at Planet Toronto. He was in the city all day."

"And we've got a picture of the guy," said Tom, flipping back to the page for Carl Russell.

Josh looked at him. "What now?"

"What now," said Tom, "is we fire this across to Lauren and Allie. They were there. If they can remember seeing him, we're on our way! Icarus is going down!"

Toronto, Canada
Monday, July 30, 5:30 P.M.

Lauren had been pacing up and down for ten minutes when finally the photography store clerk came out with an envelope in her hand and said, "There you go. Same-day developing!"

"Thanks," said Lauren.

Not even stopping to open the envelope of photographs, she raced off back down Yonge Street toward her apartment. When she'd seen Josh and Tom's note that morning, the film had still been on the kitchen table waiting to be developed.

Now it was done. Neither she nor Allie had recognized the picture of the slim, fair-haired Carl Russell—but that didn't mean a thing. There'd been stacks of people near the Meteor. He could have been one of them. And if they had photographed him . . .

Bursting through the door, she raced into the living room. Ripping open the envelope, she dumped out the photographs.

They'd come out well. Every one of them was beautifully clear, from the first shot of the yellow blob that

Allie had seen, right through to the scenes around the Meteor at the time of the safety run.

Again and again she looked at them all, until Allie finally said, "There isn't any sign of him, Lauren."

For a final time Lauren looked at the photo of herself and Silver, the unpleasant park character with the tunic and high-browed mask she'd asked to be photographed with. Dozens of people were milling in the background.

"That was taken only seconds before the crash," she said. "If any of them would have had him in, this would have been the one."

With a sigh, she tossed the photo back onto the pile. Her e-mail to Josh and Tom was short.

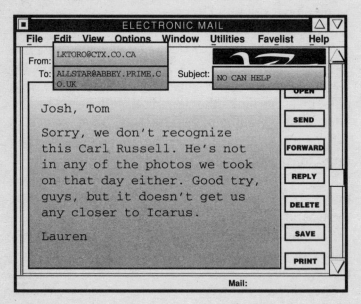

INTERNET DETECTIVES

CHAPTER 7

Delray Sun Hotel, Florida
Tuesday, July 31, 9:30 A.M.

Tamsyn and Rob eased open the door of the Delray Sun Hotel's business suite. A man was seated at the PC, his collar open and his tie loosened.

"Out of luck," whispered Tamsyn.

Rob nodded. They were just about to leave when the man muttered, "Doggone thing. How anybody can understand these things, I just don't know."

Rob and Tamsyn exchanged smiles. As Tamsyn held the door open, Rob pushed through into the business suite.

"We know a bit about PCs," said Rob brightly. "Maybe we can help. . . ."

Twenty minutes later, as the businessman left with a contented whistle and his e-mails sent on their way, Rob and Tamsyn settled down at the keyboard.

"Nothing," said Tamsyn as they saw the completely empty mail log.

"Maybe they've caught him," said Rob.

"If that was the case, then Josh would *definitely* have e-mailed us," said Tamsyn. She looked at Rob. "Maybe he got fed up with full-time Net surfing and went to the beach to do some real surfing!"

Rob shook his head. "Josh? No way! Bet you a dollar he's on-line right now."

Tamsyn laughed. "You're on! Trouble is, how do we prove it one way or the other?"

"Well . . . ," said Rob.

Without saying any more, he swept the cursor up to the menu item Utilities, then on to Talk in the drop-down menu. Immediately a question appeared in the center of the screen.

```
TALK TO WHICH USER ID?
```

"Let's see what happens to this." Rob grinned as he typed:

```
ALLSTAR@ABBEY.PRIME.CO.UK
```

Manor House
Tuesday, July 31, 2:35 P.M.

Josh and Tom read Lauren's reply with disappointment. Even though it had been a long shot, Carl Russell *had* looked to be a likely candidate for Icarus.

"No use," said Tom. "As my dad's always saying, without positive identification you get nowhere fast."

It was at that moment that the Talk request from Rob came in.

TALK> REQUEST FROM GUEST_X@DELRAY.COM
ANSWER Y OR N:

"Definitely!" yelled Josh as he typed "Y."

Delray Sun Hotel, Florida
Tuesday, July 31, 9:40 A.M.

Tamsyn cast an anxious glance toward the door of the business suite.

"Somebody's going to come along here if he doesn't answer quickly. . . ."

"You owe me a dollar," teased Rob as Josh's reply flicked up on the screen.

TALK> REQUEST ACCEPTED BY
ALLSTAR@ABBEY.PRIME.CO.UK

Rob started typing. Every time he finished a sentence, he clicked on the Send button. At the other end, he knew, Josh would do the same.

```
Hi, Josh. Tom there with you?

   JOSH> Yep, he's here. Can't keep a good
   Aussie away from the surf!

Any news on Icarus? Has he come up with
another warning?

   JOSH> Yeah, number 3. It's the biggie. He's
   after a million dollars. If Planet
   Excitement doesn't agree to pay by Thursday,
   that's it.
```

What a kook! Any idea why he's doing it?

> JOSH> He thinks Planet Excitement stole one
> of his ideas for a theme-park ride. Knowing
> that, we thought — okay, dreamed — we might
> have identified him yesterday! We found him
> by accident, but he fits the bill something
> fierce — right down to a "flying saucer"
> ride he's thought up. He's a flight
> attendant by the name of Russell.

As they saw this, Tamsyn and Rob exchanged glances.

"Flight attendant?" said Tamsyn.

Rob's next line almost typed itself, his fingers moved so quickly across the keyboard.

Russell. Do you know what his first name is?

> JOSH> Carl. Why?

Because there was a flight attendant on our
plane coming over who was called Carl. *And*
he said he was going to be flying the Canada
route last weekend!

> JOSH> Russell was flying to Toronto, too!
> He's a real Net user, got a sort of mini-
> diary on-line for his contacts to look at.
> Hey, and there's a picture of him there as
> well. Can you check it out? Get into
> Science Fiction, then search on "ride."
> You'll get his article. Click on his name
> and you'll get his picture.

Okay. Will do. If he's the same guy, we'll get
back to you in the next couple of minutes.

Signing off from their Talk session, Rob and Tamsyn followed Josh's instructions.

Soon they were staring at the photograph of Carl Russell on the screen.

"It *is* him," said Tamsyn. "Look, he's even wearing the same style uniform he was wearing on the plane coming over."

"A guy who was in the right place at the right time," said Rob. "And who's posted an idea about a theme-park ride on the Net. It's *got* to be him!"

Manor House
Tuesday, July 31, 2:43 P.M.

"Come on, come on," muttered Tom.

Suddenly the Talk request panel popped up in the middle of the screen again. Quickly Josh set up the connection.

```
    ROB> It's the same guy!

You're sure?

    ROB> Absolutely certain. Hey, and there's
    another thing about him. Tamsyn spotted it
    when we were on the plane. He's got a wing
    tattoo on the back of his right hand. You
    know, wing — as in Icarus!

That's got to be the clincher! Leave it to us.
```

"What can we do, though?" asked Tom as Josh disconnected the Talk session again.

"Tell your dad, for starters," said Josh. "And fire off a note to Interpol. If they know Russell's real e-mail address, they can go to his Net server company and track him down in no time."

Tom nodded enthusiastically. "Right!"

Josh started working through the Net menus again. "What are you up to?" asked Tom.

"Checking out his diary. He may have updated it." The screen came up. "Yes—he has!"

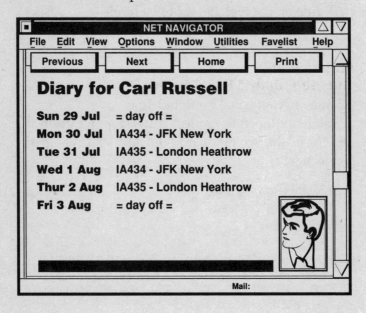

NET NAVIGATOR	△ ▽

File Edit View Options Window Utilities Favelist Help

Previous	Next	Home	Print

Diary for Carl Russell

Sun 29 Jul	= day off =
Mon 30 Jul	IA434 - JFK New York
Tue 31 Jul	IA435 - London Heathrow
Wed 1 Aug	IA434 - JFK New York
Thur 2 Aug	IA435 - London Heathrow
Fri 3 Aug	= day off =

Mail:

"So on Wednesday he'll be heading for New York!" said Tom.

Josh leaped to his feet. "What are we waiting for, Tom? Let's go call your dad and tell him what we know."

"Sure thing!" Tom leaped to his feet, too—then sat down again, a thoughtful look on his face. "Hang on. Let's just think about this for a minute."

Josh frowned. "What is there to think about? We can tell the police who Icarus is, and where he's going to be!"

"But . . . wouldn't it be even better if we could tell them how to catch him *in the act*?"

"In the act?" echoed Josh.

"Red-handed!" Tom's eyes were shining. "Dad says that's the best by a mile. Catch the crook with his fingers in the till and there's *no* way he can deny it!"

Not for the first time, Josh found himself struggling to work out what Tom was thinking. "Okay, spill it. What's going on in that Perth brain of yours?"

"This," said Tom slowly. "Icarus says he's going to send his final note to the Planet Excitement people on Wednesday the first, right?"

"Right." Josh nodded.

"And if we're right, and this Carl Russell *is* Icarus, then we know where he's going to be on that day, right?" He pointed at Russell's diary entry for that day, still on the glowing screen.

Wed 1 Aug IA434 - JFK New York

"In New York."

"So," said Josh, "you think that's where he's going to be sending his final warning from? New York?"

"Has to be, doesn't it?" said Tom. He held a finger in

the air. "Now then, think about it. Where does it look like he's sending all his messages from?"

"Cyber-cafés," said Josh, remembering what Mr. Peterson had told them the police had discovered. Suddenly he understood. "You're not thinking . . ."

Tom grinned widely. "Of Mitch and Cyber-Snax? You bet I am! Think about it, Josh. Icarus turns up there all unsuspecting, gets halfway through typing his final message, and—whammo! Mitch nabs him! It's perfect!"

"It's crazy!"

"No, it isn't."

Josh shook his head. "Yes, it is! Tom—New York is a pretty big place. Like, *massive*. There must be a million cyber-cafés there. How do you know Icarus will go to Cyber-Snax? And if he doesn't, if he sends his warning note from somewhere else, what then?"

"Then it'll be on the Net before his plane takes off on Thursday morning," said Tom coolly. "We tell the police then, and they'll be waiting to clap him in handcuffs the minute his plane touches down in London."

"Okay," said Josh. "But you still haven't told me how you know he'll go to Cyber-Snax."

"I don't," said Tom with an infuriating smile.

"So what makes you so certain he *will* go there, then?" yelled Josh.

"Because there's a good chance he doesn't know *any* cyber-cafés at all in the area. If that's the case, then there's an equally good chance he'll turn up at Cyber-Snax if it's the first one he finds out about."

"And how do you plan to make *that* happen?"

"No problem," said Tom. Reaching for the mouse, he opened an e-mail they'd laughed about earlier.

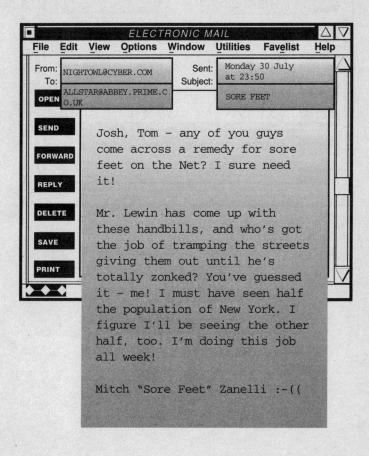

Tom clicked on Reply. Within seconds, their request was on its way.

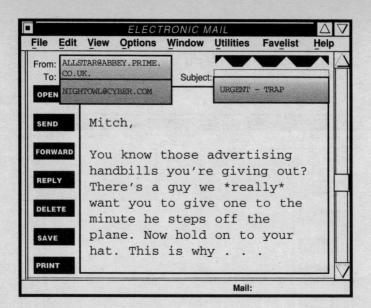

INTERNET DETECTIVES

CHAPTER 8

Cyber-Snax Café, New York
Wednesday, August 1, 7:30 A.M.

Mitch strode into the café with as determined a stride as he could manage after tramping the streets of New York for two days. He'd made up his mind. His job at Cyber-Snax was as a Net assistant and table clearer, not as a street-tramper! And that was just what he was going to tell Mr. Lewin.

His boss was in the back room, his head bent over some complicated-looking accounts.

"Hey, Mr. Lewin," said Mitch at once. "Any chance I can pass on the handbills today?"

Mr. Lewin looked up. "Why's that?"

"I don't think it's such a good idea," said Mitch, wading into the speech he'd been rehearsing as he walked. "People just take a handbill from me, then right away they dump it in the trash can further down the street. It's a waste of good money, Mr. Lewin. You'd do better to put them on the counter and ask the customers to take one for a friend."

Mitch's boss looked down thoughtfully at his books. "Let me finish up here first, Mitch. I'll be with you just as soon as I'm done."

Feeling as though he'd made his point, Mitch wandered out into the café area and sat down at a PC. They didn't open for another half hour. At least he could get in thirty minutes of surfing before work started. He clicked on the computer and logged onto the Net.

The note from Tom and Josh was waiting for him.

"Catch Icarus red-handed?" he murmured as he read it. "Man, do I like that idea!"

He'd just finished when Mr. Lewin came out from the back room. "Mitch, I've been thinking about what you said. I think you could be right. Business doesn't seem to have increased. So let's forget about the handbills today, all right?"

"Forget about them?" said Mitch. What had he done, talking Mr. Lewin out of continuing his handbills scheme? Now he was going to have to talk him back *into* it again!

"Not go out, you mean?" said Mitch, playing for time. "You sure about that, Mr. Lewin?"

"I thought that's what you were suggesting," said Mitch's boss, looking confused.

"No way, Mr. Lewin!" Mitch thought furiously. "No, what I meant was . . . gee, it must have come out all wrong . . . what I was trying to say was that we're . . . we're giving those handbills out to the wrong people!"

Mr. Lewin's eyebrows dipped. "The wrong people?"

"Yeah. I figure the person we want to catch isn't

your regular New Yorker. They've probably got their own PCs at home. We want to hit a different bunch of people."

"Such as?" said Mr. Lewin.

This was it. Mitch took a deep breath. "Visitors, Mr. Lewin. Net-surfers on a trip to New York."

Even as his boss thought about it, Mitch was getting to his feet. "The airport, Mr. Lewin. That's where I want to be today. The airport!"

Flight IA434
Wednesday, August 1
1:08 P.M. New York time

Carl Russell settled himself into the seat near the emergency exit and fastened his seat belt.

The anticipation had been building up ever since they'd taken off from London. Soon he would be sending his final message.

Then the Planet Excitement Corporation would know.

Then they would *have* to make a decision.

Either they paid him the money he was owed—or on Friday they would regret it.

As the plane touched down with a gentle bump and a muffled screech of its wheels, Carl Russell undid his seat belt. Find a cyber-café—that was the first thing he had to do.

John F. Kennedy Airport, New York
Wednesday, August 1, 1:48 P.M.

The voice on the loudspeaker was sharp and clear.

"International Airways announces the arrival of flight IA four thirty-four from London, Heathrow."

Mitch moved toward the arrivals gate. He glanced again at the picture of the slim, fair-haired man he was looking for, downloaded from the Net and printed out before he'd left Cyber-Snax. In his mind, he ran through the other things Tom and Josh had told him in their note.

```
His name is Carl Russell, Mitch. He's a flight
attendant for International Airways and should
be on flight IA434 from London. According to
the schedule, it gets into JFK at about 1:45
p.m.
Apart from the photograph from his own page on
the Net, the only other thing we know about
Russell is that he's got a wing tattooed on
the back of one hand. It should be easy to
check that when you give him one of your
Cyber-Snax handbills!
```

Mitch adjusted the bundle of handbills he'd taken from Mr. Lewin's box. There were a lot more than he needed, but he had a reason for taking that many.

He looked around. The airport was in its usual hectic state, with passengers and airline crews scurrying about. Mitch noticed a stocky policeman leaning casually against a phone booth, surveying the area. *He's about the only person who isn't racing somewhere!* he thought.

A woman emerged from the arrivals gate pushing her luggage on a trolley. Noticing the bright blue and red *IA* label dangling from the top suitcase, Mitch moved right across to the narrow exit through which every passenger would have to pass.

Mitch plucked a handbill from his pile and handed it to the woman as she reached him. "Cyber-Snax, *the* Internet café," he said brightly. "Surf while you sip!"

Other passengers were coming out now. Mitch got ready to give them leaflets, too. Although he didn't expect the cabin crew to come out for a while yet, he couldn't be certain. If Russell did appear in the middle of a group of passengers, it was important that he should see Mitch giving everybody a Cyber-Snax leaflet. The last thing he wanted was for Russell to suspect that he was being singled out for special treatment.

But as he plucked another leaflet from his pile, Mitch felt a strong hand grab his arm.

"No soliciting, kid!"

It was the stocky police officer Mitch had last seen leaning against a phone booth—and he had a scowl on his face that clearly said he wasn't in a good mood.

"Hey, give me a break," said Mitch.

"Forget it. Passengers don't want handbills stuck up their noses the minute they get off a plane."

"But my boss sent me to give these out. He'll be real mad at me if I don't do it."

"And I'll be real mad at you if you do," growled the cop. "So, which do you want?"

"Just for a while," pleaded Mitch.

The cop didn't even bother to shake his head. "Scram!"

Mitch didn't know what to do. One false move and the cop would be after him. But if he went outside, where the cop couldn't see him, he'd have a bigger problem. The airport concourse had dozens of exits. Russell could leave by any one of them. No, the only way to guarantee that he'd get to him was by staying here and watching the arrivals gate.

Or is it? wondered Mitch as the loudspeaker crackled with another announcement. Its tinny voice had given him an idea.

Keeping his eye on the stream of people now coming through the arrivals gate, Mitch drifted across to a kiosk in the middle of the concourse. A large sign above it read Information Desk.

A crowd of passengers was milling around this desk, their suitcases at their feet. Behind the counter, trying to deal with a battery of requests, were two harassed-looking assistants.

Mitch eased himself into a spot at the far end of the counter. Just behind it stood a microphone on a low stand. Every so often one of the assistants, a young woman in a light blue uniform, would head his way and use the microphone to put a call out over the loudspeaker. Usually it was a request for a person meeting a passenger to come to the desk.

Finally the woman got to Mitch. "Can I help you?" she said.

Mitch looked over at the arrivals gate. A little group

of white-shirted cabin crew members had just pushed through. One of them was fair-haired. Was it Russell? He had to take the chance.

"Yeah, please," said Mitch, hoisting his pile of handbills onto the counter. "Could you page someone for me? I'm supposed to be meeting my boss's pal, but I think I've missed him. Name of Russell. Mr. Russell. From England."

The woman leaned toward the microphone. "Would Mr. Russell from England please come to the information desk? Mr. Russell."

Mitch looked over toward the arrivals gate again. Would it work? What if the fair-haired man he'd seen wasn't Russell? But as the announcement echoed out over the concourse, Mitch saw the man look up. Then, suitcase in hand, he started to head their way.

Within seconds he was at the desk. "Hi. My name's Carl Russell. You paged me."

The assistant pointed down to the end of the counter, where Mitch was still standing. "Your contact is waiting for you, Mr. Russell."

Russell's face clouded over. "Contact? What contact?"

Now for the tricky part, thought Mitch as the white-shirted flight attendant came toward him.

"I'm Carl Russell. Do I know you?"

Mitch put on the blankest look. "Sorry?"

"The information woman said you paged me."

"Your name's Russell?" Looking at the harassed woman, now dealing with yet another question, Mitch shook his head and sighed. He leaned over the counter, pushing to one side the pile of Cyber-Snax leaflets he'd carefully placed there. "Excuse me, miss. I said Russo! My boss's pal, Mr. Russo!"

He turned back to Russell. "Gee, I'm sorry. I'll get her to call again."

Immediately he saw that the flight attendant wasn't paying full attention to him. His eye caught by the startling orange of the Cyber-Snax handbills, Russell was looking down at them.

Take one! urged Mitch, as if sheer thought power could do the trick. *This is an information desk! It's information!*

Russell started to leave. Then, with the slightest of pauses, he plucked the top handbill from the pile.

Mitch left the concourse himself twenty minutes later, after the poor woman had tried three times to summon the nonexistent Mr. Russo on the loudspeaker.

So now at least Russell knew about Cyber-Snax. And he *was* Russell, there was no doubt about that. The photograph on the Net had been a little old. Russell wasn't as slim as he'd expected, and his hair had darkened slightly.

But there was one thing about him that had been dead on—the tattoo he'd seen on the back of his hand as he took the Cyber-Snax leaflet. Mitch had seen the angel's wing quite clearly.

Central Park, New York
6:45 P.M.

Russell eased himself off the park bench. He'd been sitting and thinking about what he would write. Now it was clear in his mind.

This, his final note as Icarus, would tell them exactly where and when he would strike. That way they would be in no doubt about how confident he was that he could avoid capture.

It was their fault. He had written to them with details of his ideas. He'd sent them pages of information. What had he received in reply? A standard letter, thanking him for his interest and saying that his letter would be "kept on file." *Kept on file!* He knew what that meant. Ditched! If they'd kept it, they would have known who he was. But obviously they hadn't kept his letter.

As far as Carl Russell was concerned, what they *had* done was very clear. They'd simply stolen his idea and paid nothing for it.

Well, now he was asking for what was rightfully his: a share of the profits that his idea would bring them . . . enough money to allow him to give up the job he hated and devote all his talents to his inventions. Surely they would agree.

He hoped so. He would not enjoy having to carry out his threat. But, if it was necessary, he *would* do it.

With another glance at the address on the bright orange leaflet, Carl Russell stood up and began walking.

Cyber-Snax Café
6:55 P.M.

As Mitch saw Russell open the door, he edged his way quickly into the back room.

Mr. Lewin looked up. "I told you when you got back, Mitch. The ones you took with you were the last of the handbills. No more until I get another batch printed."

Mitch didn't need telling. That was why he'd taken so many—every last one, in fact. To make sure that he was in the café if and when Carl Russell turned up.

And now here he was!

"Mr. Lewin," whispered Mitch. "Don't ask me to explain. Just listen. There's a guy who just came in who's a blackmailer. His name's Carl Russell. Interpol is after him. I managed to give him one of your leaflets at the airport. He's gonna send a ransom note to the Planet Excitement Corporation right now."

At his small desk, Mr. Lewin could only stare openmouthed. Finally he found the words. "Mitch—are you off your rocker?"

"Honest, Mr. Lewin!"

Mitch cast an anxious glance out into the café. Another assistant had taken Russell's money and seated him at the PC nearest the door.

"Look," continued Mitch urgently, "can you call the cops? Get them here fast, before he leaves."

Mr. Lewin stretched a hand toward the phone, then paused. "If this is some kind of game . . ."

"It isn't! You've got to believe me!"

Mitch's boss paused for a moment longer. Then he

snatched up the phone and began punching in a number.

Anxiously Mitch darted to the doorway, from where he could see into the café. Russell's head was down as he concentrated hard on what he was doing. Behind him, Mitch heard Mr. Lewin speaking.

"Yeah, yeah. Guy named Russell. Sending notes to the Planet Excitement people. Interpol wants him."

There was a pause as he listened to what the police officer on the other end of the line was saying. Then he put the receiver to his chest and turned to Mitch.

"Says he's got the Interpol fax right in front of him, and it doesn't mention any Carl Russell."

"Icarus!" cried Mitch loudly. "Tell him Icarus!"

The moment he said it, Mitch knew he'd made a mistake. As his cry of "Icarus!" carried into the café, Russell looked up.

Startled, the blackmailer looked around him—and saw Mitch standing at the back room door. A look of recognition came into his eyes. At that instant, Mitch felt he could read his mind. He was putting the facts together—seeing Mitch at the airport, the Cyber-Snax handbills, the call for a Mr. Russell . . . and now the shout of his code name.

Russell leaped to his feet and was out of the door before Mitch could move.

Mitch went after him along West 111th Street and then turned right onto Adam Clayton Powell Jr. Boulevard.

At the end of the block Russell slowed as he approached the busy Central Park North thoroughfare, his head darting from side to side as he searched for a gap in the speeding traffic.

Mitch closed on him. Russell saw him coming and frantically scanned the road once more. Suddenly the merest of gaps appeared. With Mitch no more than fifteen feet away, Russell launched himself forward and into the road.

Mitch didn't stop to think. He raced into the road himself—only to hear a terrifying squeal of brakes. He looked to the side. A yellow cab, its driver gritting his teeth as he tried to stop, was almost on top of him. Leaping back to the curb, Mitch tumbled to safety as the cab came to a halt on the very spot where he'd been.

By the time he got to his feet again, Russell was across the road and racing into the safe cover of Central Park.

The rest of the evening passed in a blur. Even while Mitch had been giving chase, Mr. Lewin had been on the line with the New York Police Department. It seemed that no sooner had Mitch got back to the café than a squad car was wailing toward it.

Mitch was quizzed at length about what had happened.

"Come on, he'll get away!" he'd had to urge more than once, until finally the police officers were convinced about what he was telling them.

Soon the place was crawling with uniformed officers and detectives, newspaper and TV reporters following hot on their heels as the news spread.

"That is correct," said one detective as a reporter

asked him to confirm that Russell's hotel room had been found empty. "It took a while for International Airways to confirm Russell's identity and tell us which layover hotel he was at. By the time our people got there, he'd left."

"You mean you haven't got him yet?" asked Mitch.

"He won't get far. JFK airport is staked out thoroughly. He wasn't due out until tomorrow, remember. He's probably roaming the streets right now. We'll have him."

"I hope so," said Mitch. "That guy is trouble."

He looked over toward the PC that Carl Russell had been sitting at, now being dusted for fingerprints. Still glowing on the screen was the message he'd completed but not had time to send.

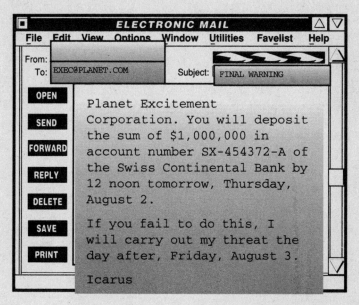

"End of story," said Mr. Lewin when they were finally left alone. "End of Icarus."

"You think so?" said Mitch.

"With what you've told them?" Mr. Lewin shook his head. "He's got no place to run, Mitch. No place at all."

As his boss went off to finish the accounts he'd started hours before, Mitch sat down to e-mail Josh and Tom.

"I just hope everybody's right," he muttered.

Manor House
Thursday, August 2, 10:25 A.M.

"They didn't get him?" cried Tom.

On the other end of the telephone line, Mr. Peterson sounded as though he was shaking his head. "Not yet."

After seeing Mitch's e-mail when they arrived at Manor House, Tom had phoned his father at the Sherriot Hotel to discover if there had been any further developments.

"But what about the money?" said Tom. "What are the Planet Excitement people going to do if he hasn't been caught by tomorrow?"

"Nothing," said Mr. Peterson. "They're being advised not to pay."

"But if he isn't caught," said Tom hotly, "he could still carry out his threat. I mean, he could be *anywhere!*"

"Not anywhere," said Mr. Peterson. "It seems Mr. Russell had a contingency plan, just in case something went wrong. He must have jumped straight on an airport bus and gone to La Guardia."

"La Guardia?" said Tom. "Where's that?"

"Not where. What. There are two big airports in New York—Kennedy is one, and La Guardia is the other. Even if they'd gone after him right away, they wouldn't have gone to La Guardia until they'd checked out Kennedy."

"You mean he's left the country?" cried Tom. "He could be back in England?"

Josh filled in the gaps from what he'd heard. "Planet London!" he shouted. "He could be going for Planet London!"

Even at the other end of the line, Mr. Peterson heard him clearly. "Tell Josh not to worry, Tom. Your trip on Saturday's still safe. Russell hasn't left America. The flight he took was an internal one. From New York to Miami."

Manor House
11:35 A.M.

They forwarded Mitch's note about what had taken place at Cyber-Snax to Tamsyn and Rob, adding their own update at the end.

"Better copy it to Lauren as well," said Tom as Josh was typing.

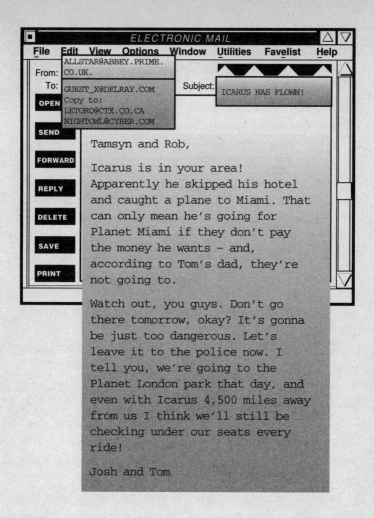

File   Edit   View   Options   Window   Utilities   Favelist   Help

From: ALLSTAR@ABBEY.PRIME.
CO.UK.

To: GUEST_X@DELRAY.COM
Copy to:
LKTORO@CTX.CO.CA
NIGHTOWL@CYBER.COM

Subject: ICARUS HAS FLOWN!

OPEN
SEND
FORWARD
REPLY
DELETE
SAVE
PRINT

Tamsyn and Rob,

Icarus is in your area!
Apparently he skipped his hotel
and caught a plane to Miami. That
can only mean he's going for
Planet Miami if they don't pay
the money he wants - and,
according to Tom's dad, they're
not going to.

Watch out, you guys. Don't go
there tomorrow, okay? It's gonna
be just too dangerous. Let's
leave it to the police now. I
tell you, we're going to the
Planet London park that day, and
even with Icarus 4,500 miles away
from us I think we'll still be
checking under our seats every
ride!

Josh and Tom

"You know Tamsyn and Rob better than me," said
Tom. "Will they do as they're told?"

"I hope so," said Josh seriously. "I really hope so."

"Oh, no!"

No sooner had Tamsyn put her head around the door to the business suite than she jerked it back again.

"What's the problem?" said Rob from behind her.

"The place is absolutely *crawling* with gray suits!"

"One of which is probably being worn by your father," said a laughing voice coming along the corridor.

"Morning, Mrs. Zanelli. What's going on?"

"We've just heard that one of our major customers has flown into Miami unexpectedly. Rob's dad is trying to e-mail him to set up a meeting. Trouble is, so is every other businessman in the hotel!"

"Not much chance of us getting on-line today, then," said Rob quietly.

Mrs. Zanelli looked at him sharply. "I didn't know you'd been using the business suite."

Rob grinned. "Special permission, Mom! No sweat—we'll pass on it today."

"Good idea," said Mrs. Zanelli. "Spend some time thinking about what you want to do tomorrow. If this meeting gets fixed up, we'll be leaving you to your own devices."

Tamsyn and Rob exchanged knowing glances. "Easy," said Rob at once. "Just drop us off at Planet Miami."

Toronto
Thursday, August 2, 11:45 A.M.

Lauren read the note from Josh and Tom and sighed. If Icarus was in Miami, then that was that. She'd had her chance to spot him and blown it.

Yet again she pulled out the photographs they'd taken while they were at Planet Toronto.

Once more she riffled through them. Once more she stopped and stared at the picture of herself and Silver the alien, surrounded by the milling crowds, taken just moments before the Meteor had crashed.

Was there a clue staring her in the face here, something she and Allie had overlooked?

No. She'd been through it in her head a dozen times. With a sigh, Lauren tucked the pictures back into their envelope.

Icarus was in Miami. The police were on his trail. She had to accept it. Her part in this particular mystery was over.

Downtown Miami
Thursday, August 2, 12 noon

The solemn voice at the other end of the line told him what he'd expected to hear.

"Your account, monsieur, has a balance of one thousand eight hundred and seventy Swiss francs. That is, one thousand three hundred dollars."

"Thank you."

Carl Russell put the receiver back slowly. Outside

the telephone booth, the bustling Miami street might not have been there. He was in his own world.

Thirteen hundred dollars. Just thirteen hundred—the amount he had deposited when he opened the account two months ago. The Planet Excitement Corporation had *not* obeyed his instructions.

Very well. They would learn that he was a man who could be relied on to keep his word.

They would not catch him. He had thought everything out far too carefully for that to happen. He would go to a drugstore and buy a bottle of hair dye. He would also buy a pair of spectacles. With them, and his fair hair dyed black, he would then find a photo booth.

He took his passport from his pocket and smiled. His name would be known by now, of course. They would be looking out for it.

He looked down at the printed wording: "Carl Russell." A simple matter. He could do it himself with a pen. Neatly top off the U to turn it into an O; add another O to the end of his first name and an I to the end of his last name, and he would be Carlo Rosselli. His handwritten signature could be altered in the same way.

Carl Russell stalked angrily away to continue with the task he had set himself.

Two hours later, he was striding confidently past a pair of unsuspecting police officers and into Miami International Airport.

CHAPTER 10

Planet London theme park
Friday, August 3, 10:10 A.M.

The bus pulled smoothly into the already crowded parking lot. In the distance, Josh could see the line stretching back from the entrance.

"Bus*y*!" said Tom.

"No reason why it shouldn't be," said Josh. "Not with Icarus out of the way."

The news about Icarus, who he was, and the fact that Interpol was searching for him in Miami had been on the evening news the day before.

"Even so," said Tom, "this is mega busy! It wouldn't surprise me if something's going on we don't know about."

They clambered out of their seats and followed Mr. and Mrs. Peterson down the aisle to join the rest of the group and get their admission tickets.

"We won't cramp your style, kids," said Mrs. Peterson as they walked toward the line at the entrance. "Once we're inside, we'll leave you two to go your own way."

"Just make sure you check in with us," said Mr. Peterson. "Say, two o'clock at the information office. Okay?"

"Okay," said Tom. He gave a disgusted look at the line snaking out in front of them. "Assuming we actually get in by two."

Mr. Peterson gave a grunt of satisfaction. "Security precautions. That's what's slowing things up. They're checking bags. And there's a couple of armed police up there, too. Probably more inside."

"What for?" said Tom. "Russell's four and a half thousand miles away."

"But I bet he's given the Planet Excitement people a real fright," said Mr. Peterson. "They're obviously taking no chances—just in case the publicity's given anybody else some funny ideas."

Slowly the line inched forward. Every so often one of the park's resident aliens would come out through the gates to wander up and down, shaking hands and posing for pictures. Then, after a while, they'd go back in again.

"Too bad we don't look like him," said Tom, pointing out a character with two heads. "Get in a lot quicker, wouldn't we?"

"Yeah," said Josh. "Hey, why don't we try squeezing ourselves into one shirt? That might work!"

Laughing, Tom shook his head. "Easier to go buy a roll of aluminum foil," he said, nudging Josh as another character walked past. "Then they might have mistaken us for him."

They watched as the character in a shiny silver tunic, its high-browed silver mask completely covering its face, marched up to the entrance.

Then, without pausing, it walked past the security check and into the Planet London theme park.

Beneath his mask, Carl Russell smiled to himself. The fools! Did they think they could stop him? They weren't even looking in the right country!

The scene in New York had been disturbing. He didn't know how anyone had recognized him. But he'd outsmarted them nevertheless.

His change of identity had worked. His altered passport, flashed in front of busy officials just minutes before the final call for takeoff, had got him through, as he knew it would.

Once in London, he'd only had to go to his small apartment to pick up the equipment he needed. . . .

And now he was here. This was the day. If they'd thought about it at all, the Planet Excitement people would have been able to work out that here was where the disaster *had* to happen.

Where it *would* happen.

Lauren's apartment, Toronto
8:10 A.M. (UK time 1:10 P.M.)

Lauren hadn't slept very well. All through the night she'd jerked awake as the thought that she'd missed something nagged at her. Climbing out of bed, she padded into the living room and turned on her PC.

Maybe there was something on the Net she'd overlooked. It only took a few moments for her to surf through to the details about Carl Russell.

```
E-mail address: carlruss@interair.co.uk
Occupation: Flight attendant, International
Airways
Hobbies, interests: Flying, space travel,
science fiction.
```

"Science fiction," murmured Lauren, looking again at Russell's hobbies and interests. *Nothing there, right? That's why he came up with his idea for Planet Excitement.* She read on.

I think space exploration has brought about many benefits. I'm certain there's life on other planets, and think it's very likely that Earth has been visited by UFOs. I read a lot of science fiction books, and you could well bump into me at meetings of the Science Fiction Society.

Science Fiction Society? Lauren turned as Allie came in, balancing a cup with a saucer on top. "What do you think goes on at the Science Fiction Society?"

Lauren's grandmother thought for a moment, then, chuckling, moved her hand up and down. "Play with flying saucers?"

"Allie! Be serious!"

Alice put her cup down on the sideboard. "I don't know. Talk about books, watch films, read magazines, dress up . . ."

"What? What do you mean, dress up?"

"Like I say, dress up. It happens all the time. I was sailing the Net the other day and found this English History Society. They get dressed up as Cavaliers and Roundheads and go out weekends to have pretend battles."

Furiously Lauren dived for the photographs of their day at Planet Toronto. There it was. It had been staring at her all the time.

"Silver!" she cried.

Alice looked her way. "Huh?"

"Silver. The unpleasant alien character at Planet Toronto. He'd just got off the Meteor when we saw him, Allie. It could have been him who planted that explosive device. He could be Icarus."

Silently but quickly her grandmother reached into a drawer of the sideboard and pulled out a magnifying glass. Kneeling down next to Lauren, she squinted hard at the photograph.

"If you're looking for a tattoo, forget it, Allie. He's got gloves on."

"I wasn't," said Lauren's grandmother. She lifted her head and tapped at the waistband around the character's silver tunic. "I was looking at that. I'd assumed it was a two-way radio, like all the others had."

"And isn't it?"

"No. It hasn't got a speaker. I think it's a radio control box. The sort Icarus would have needed to use to set off that explosion . . ."

There was no time to lose. Lauren leaped to the keyboard and began pounding out a note.

"I've got to let them know, Allie. I just hope they haven't left."

"Who?"

"Tamsyn and Rob, of course. They assume Icarus is in Miami, remember?"

Planet London
1:30 P.M.

The ride was everything he'd imagined it to be.

From the outside, it looked like a large flying saucer. He'd boarded it by walking up the ramp, dozens of excited youngsters in front of and behind him.

The seats inside had been arranged in a circle, each seat facing one of the portholes. He'd taken his seat, tightening the belt across his lap.

The ramp closed with a quiet clunk. For a moment there was silence, no movement. Then they began to spin. Outside, the world whirled by.

He knew what was coming next. Hadn't it been *his* idea in the first place? Still spinning, their craft began to move along a track. As it gathered speed it also tilted as the track went steeply upward. Faster and faster it moved, up and up. Outside the portholes there appeared a backdrop of stars and planets, giving him the sensation that he really was flying through space.

And then it happened. A voice over the craft's speaker system cried out, "Emergency! Quantum leap!"

In an instant everything went black and, now spinning even faster, the craft began to plummet down-ward.

Terrified screams tore through the air as, without be-ing able to see or hear, everybody was gripped by the sensation of falling. And then, when it seemed as though it would never end, it was as if they'd sud-denly landed on a feather cushion.

The real world reappeared outside the portholes. They saw the faces of those lining up for the next turn on the ride.

And the voice over the speaker was saying, "Thank you, crew. You have survived the Quantum Leap. Be proud. Tell your friends. Can they face the challenge of the Quantum Leap?"

My idea. They stole it.

He'd realized that the moment he'd read the news-paper articles about the new ride the Planet Excite-ment Corporation was developing.

Carl Russell eased the small, round container from the baggy pocket of his silver tunic. Sliding it under-neath his seat, he felt the pull as its magnetic surface clamped onto the metal seat support.

He stood up. The explosive was in place. All he had to do now was detonate it.

Delray Sun Hotel, Florida
8:35 A.M. (UK time 1:35 P.M.)

Tamsyn looked at the notice and let out a frustrated wail. "What! Are we *ever* going to log on again?"

"Problem?" said Rob, wheeling himself down the corridor toward her.

Tamsyn pointed at the handwritten sign on the door of the business suite. " 'Computer out of order,' " she read. "Yesterday we couldn't get near it; today it's busted!"

"It was okay at eight o'clock," said Rob, easing open the door.

"How do you know?"

"Because," Rob said with a grin, "that's when I wrote the sign! Now get in here quick before somebody comes!"

"Disgraceful!" answered Tamsyn. "But I like it!" Quickly she followed Rob in, jamming a chair under the door handle for good measure.

They sat down and logged in. "Two messages," said Rob as he saw the Mail Waiting message on the status line. Together they read the note that Josh and Tom had sent, warning them not to go anywhere near Planet Miami while Icarus was still on the run.

"What are we going to do?" asked Tamsyn. "Your parents are hardly going to leave us there for the day if they know Icarus is still on the loose."

Rob looked all innocent. "They will if they don't know. And I'm not planning on mentioning it!"

Tamsyn was uncertain. "Rob, he's dangerous. If he does get in . . ." She stopped as she remembered that the police now had Russell's picture from the Net. "No, of course he won't. They know what he looks like."

"That might not help." Now Rob's voice was icy cold. He'd opened the note from Lauren.

Together they read their friend's explanation of what she and Allie had deduced, that Russell had managed to sabotage the Meteor by disguising himself as one of the characters who roamed every Planet Experience theme park.

Then they downloaded the photograph that Lauren had scanned in of herself and Russell in his silver costume.

"But you know what this means?" said Tamsyn. "He *could* sneak in, even if they've got guards on every gate. If he put that gear on outside, they wouldn't spot him."

Rob looked at her. "Then we've *got* to go to Planet Miami, Tamsyn. We've got to stop him. We've got to scour the park and find him."

"Scour the park?" echoed Tamsyn. "Rob, that place is *massive*. We only covered a fraction of it the day we were there. There's no way we could do more today. . . ."

Even as she said the words, she reached for the mouse. Perhaps there *was* a way of doing it.

"What are you looking for?" said Rob as Tamsyn came out of e-mail and went into Net Navigator. Moments later she was starting to trace through the Science menus to the notes that Carl Russell had posted in the Science Fiction section.

"What exactly *was* his idea?" said Tamsyn. "If he's so steamed up about it being stolen, then isn't that the ride he'll go for?"

Rob nodded in agreement. "The Meteor, I assume. That's the one he hit at Planet Toronto, wasn't it?"

Russell's entry flashed up on the screen.

```
A fun idea I've had is that it could make a
really good theme-park ride — a flying saucer
that floats slowly upward, then shoots back
down again, stopping on a cushion of air just
before it crashes! I think kids would love it.
```

"Rob," said Tamsyn, "that doesn't describe the Meteor. It's nothing like it."

"It's not like any of the rides we went on," said Rob, thinking back to their day at Planet Miami. "It must be describing one that we didn't get around to. We can check the guidebook."

Tamsyn shook her head. "Knowing we were going again today, I read that book again from cover to cover. It doesn't describe *any* of the rides."

It was Rob's turn to reach for the mouse. "Then maybe the guidebook's out of date," he said. "Let's try something that isn't."

Returning to the Net Navigator home page, he switched to the Entertainment menu. Within seconds he'd found the Planet Excitement Corporation home page, with its underlined entries of Planet List, Voyages, and Future Launches.

He clicked on Voyages. A list of attractions to be found at every Planet Excitement theme park came up.

"Nothing," Tamsyn said as she scanned through the descriptions of each.

"Let's try that one," said Rob, clicking on Future Launches.

"That's it!" cried Tamsyn. "That's the one! Look at the description—that's what Russell wrote."

Rob's voice sounded numb. "Then we're not going to find him. Look at the next screen."

NET NAVIGATOR

File   Edit   View   Options   Window   Utilities   Favelist   Help

Previous   Next   Home   Print

Opening dates
23rd August **Planet Toronto**
26th August **Planet Tokyo**
30th August **Planet Miami**

But if you want to be one of the first
to make a Quantum Leap...

3rd August - Planet London

Mail:

"I don't think he's in Miami at all," said Rob. "I think he's going for Planet London."

Tamsyn's heart skipped a beat. "Josh and Tom," she cried. "We've got to warn them!" She looked at her watch. "It's only nine o'clock. They might not have left yet."

Rob shook his head. "We're in Florida, remember. We're five hours behind them. In England it's two o'clock in the afternoon."

"Then there's nothing we *can* do . . .," whispered Tamsyn.

"Yes, there is," yelled Rob. "It's called the telephone. We can call them at the Planet London site. They'll page them." He pushed himself rapidly to the door. "Come on, Tamsyn! It might not be too late!"

Planet London
2:24 P.M.

"Would Josh Allan and Tom Peterson please report to the information office immediately." The page operator repeated the names. "Josh Allan and Tom Peterson."

Josh looked up at the loudspeaker mounted on the post nearby. "That's us. They're calling us."

Tom looked unconcerned. "Yeah, I heard."

"Well, aren't we going?"

"Not on your life."

"It might be important."

Tom shook his head. "Josh, it's half past two. We said we'd meet my mom and dad at two, right? Where? At the information office. It'll just be them, getting all upset."

"You're not moving, then?" said Josh.

"And lose our places after waiting here for years?" said Tom firmly. "No way."

After getting soaked on Splashdown!, the water-ride attraction nearby, they'd headed straight across to join the line they were now in. That had been nearly an hour ago. Josh looked ahead. They were almost at the front. After the next ride, they'd be on. Tom was probably right. If so, he'd be the one to get in trouble from Mr. and Mrs. Peterson!

"Here we go!" said Tom as excited shouts came from in front of them.

The line began to move. *No wonder it's as crowded as it is*, thought Josh. How they'd managed to miss the news that this was the opening day of Planet London's new attraction, he really didn't know.

Suddenly feeling the iron grille of the ramp beneath his feet, Josh realized they were there. He began climbing, with Tom beside him.

Moments later they were settling into their seats.

"Quantum Leap, huh?" said Tom. "Let's hope this ride is as good as it sounds."

Carl Russell pulled back his silver glove and checked his watch.

Yes, it was time.

After planting the device, he had walked around the park, enjoying the power he felt, knowing that at a time of his choosing he could punish the Planet Excitement Corporation for what they'd done to him.

Now it was time.

But not here, away from the attraction. He wanted to be closer. He wanted to see it happen.

He began to walk toward the high, brightly lit sign that read Quantum Leap.

The ride began.

As their craft began spinning, Josh gripped the sides of his seat. He enjoyed rides like this a lot—but only after they'd finished. While he was actually on them, he wasn't so sure.

Next to him, though, Tom looked as though he was ready to burst with excitement—and he wasn't holding on at all! Josh let go again.

They were moving upward now. Josh felt himself sliding back into his seat as they gathered speed. The stars outside the portholes were flashing by, faster and faster.

"Emergency! Quantum leap!"

Josh couldn't help himself. As everything went black and the craft began to plummet downward his hands flew down to grab hold of his seat.

That was when he felt it.

As his fingers wrapped around the sides and underneath, their tips touched something. It moved. The ride forgotten, he felt further, stretching out his hand to grip the small, round device that seemed to be stuck to the bottom of his seat.

A sudden, cushioning jerk snapped his head up. In that instant he knew what he'd found.

Icarus wasn't in Miami. He was here!

"Thank you, crew," the speaker system began to drone. "You have survived the Quantum Leap. . . ."

Carl Russell stopped. He looked up at the sign, Quantum Leap, almost above his head. This was close enough.

As he saw the space capsule end its ride, he unclipped the remote control from his belt.

Ahead, the capsule's door was opening. Its ramp was being lowered.

He would wait until they got off. That way fewer would be injured. His argument was with Planet Excitement, not the innocent children. Although *some* would be hurt, he knew that. . . .

"Fantastic, wasn't it?" cried Tom as the doors opened and the ramp slid down.

Josh didn't answer. As the lights had flicked on he'd pulled the round device from beneath his seat. He'd never seen a bomb of any size before, but if this *was* one . . .

Leaping up, he raced for the exit. Screams echoed around the chamber as he ducked out and half ran, half threw himself down the ramp.

Then he was running, running toward the one place he could think of that was safe. . . .

Mr. Peterson hit Carl Russell with the force of a runaway train, tumbling on top of the silver-suited blackmailer and knocking the remote control from his hand.

As he landed on the ground, Russell saw the control spinning just out of his reach. He lunged for it.

Desperately Mr. Peterson did the same. Their hands landed on the control at virtually the same instant.

But Russell's hand got there first.

An instant later came the sickening sound of the explosion.

As the noise rumbled through the air and a great plume of water shot up into the sky, Russell seemed to give up the struggle.

For a moment he lay on the ground. Then, softly, he began to moan. "What have I done? What have I done? I'm sorry. . . ."

Mr. Peterson looked up. Ahead of him, people were coming out of the shock the explosion had caused. Panic was setting in. Now they were running this way and that.

"Tom!" screamed Mr. Peterson. "Tom! Where are you?"

For a moment all he could see were frightened faces. Then he saw his son coming toward him, a stunned look on his face.

Mr. Peterson leaped up and clutched his son. "Tom! What happened? Are you all right?"

Tom could only shake his head. "I'm all right," he mumbled, "but Josh . . ."

"Josh? What about him?"

Tom looked around wildly. "When we got off the Quantum Leap, he had something in his hand. He just sprinted past me."

"Which way?" yelled Mr. Peterson.

"Toward that water . . ."

They saw him then, on his hands and knees near the Splashdown! ride. Tom and his father raced across.

"Josh!" cried Tom. "Are you all right?"

"No, I am not," moaned Josh. "I'm totally soaked!"

Manor House
Saturday, August 11, 9:50 A.M.

"You want me to type it?" Tom grinned. "Or have your hands stopped shaking now?"

Josh gave him a friendly scowl. "No problem, Tom—I think. . . ."

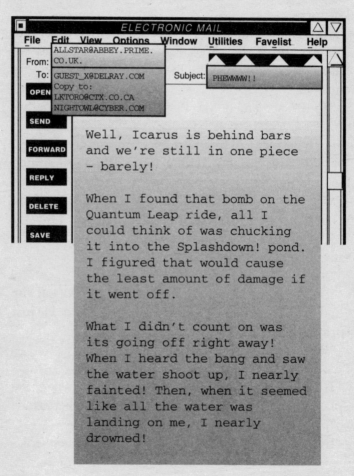

ELECTRONIC MAIL

File Edit View Options Window Utilities Favelist Help

From: ALLSTAR@ABBEY.PRIME.CO.UK.

To: GUEST_X@DELRAY.COM
Copy to:
LKTORO@CTX.CO.CA
NIGHTOWL@CYBER.COM

Subject: PHEWWWW!!

OPEN
SEND
FORWARD
REPLY
DELETE
SAVE

Well, Icarus is behind bars and we're still in one piece – barely!

When I found that bomb on the Quantum Leap ride, all I could think of was chucking it into the Splashdown! pond. I figured that would cause the least amount of damage if it went off.

What I didn't count on was its going off right away! When I heard the bang and saw the water shoot up, I nearly fainted! Then, when it seemed like all the water was landing on me, I nearly drowned!

"Move over," said Tom. "My turn."

Josh slid to one side as Tom took over at the keyboard.

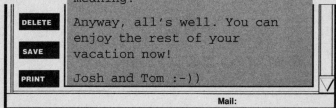

```
Hi, everyone. This is Tom
typing this bit. No, not
because Josh *has* fainted!
It's just that the next bit
concerns my dad.

Tamsyn and Rob, the reason my
dad answered your call when
they announced it over the
loudspeaker was because I
ignored it. And he went to
find out what it was all
about. After you told him
about Icarus and the Quantum
Leap ride, he shot out of
there like a bullet from a gun
- and dived on Silver the
Alien just as he was about to
blast us off, if you get my
meaning!
```

DELETE	`Anyway, all's well. You can`
	`enjoy the rest of your`
SAVE	`vacation now!`
PRINT	`Josh and Tom :-))`

Mail:

"And us," said Josh. "We can enjoy the rest of our vacation, too."

Tom grinned. "Not me, pal. I go home tomorrow, remember?"

Josh looked at the calendar on Rob's wall. It was true. Tom's two weeks were almost over.

"You think you'll come over again sometime?"

"After this?" said Tom. "No problem! Next time they have a police conference, I'm expecting them to invite me!"